Christine Merrill lives on a [...] USA, with her husband, two [...] pets—all of whom would like [...] computer so they can check their e-mail. She has worked by turns in theatre costuming and as a librarian. Writing historical romance combines her love of good stories and fancy dress with her ability to stare out of the window and make stuff up.

Also by Christine Merrill

'Unwrapped under the Mistletoe'
in *Regency Christmas Liaisons*
A Scandalous Match for the Marquess
'A Mistletoe Kiss for the Governess'
in *Regency Christmas Weddings*

Society's Most Scandalous collection

How to Survive a Scandal

Secrets of the Duke's Family miniseries

Lady Margaret's Mysterious Gentleman
Lady Olivia's Forbidden Protector
Lady Rachel's Dangerous Duke

The Irresistible Dukes miniseries

Awakening His Shy Duchess
A Duke for the Penniless Widow

Discover more at millsandboon.co.uk.

TO WED A DEVILISH DUKE

Christine Merrill

MILLS & BOON

All rights reserved including the right of reproduction in whole or in part in any form. This edition is published by arrangement with Harlequin Enterprises ULC.

This is a work of fiction. Names, characters, places, locations and incidents are purely fictional and bear no relationship to any real life individuals, living or dead, or to any actual places, business establishments, locations, events or incidents. Any resemblance is entirely coincidental.

Without limiting the author's and publisher's exclusive rights, any unauthorised use of this publication to train generative artificial intelligence (AI) technologies is expressly prohibited. HarperCollins also exercise their rights under Article 4(3) of the Digital Single Market Directive 2019/790 and expressly reserve this publication from the text and data mining exception.

® and TM are trademarks owned and used by the trademark owner and/or its licensee. Trademarks marked with ® are registered with the United Kingdom Patent Office and/or the Office for Harmonisation in the Internal Market and in other countries.

First published in Great Britain 2025
by Mills & Boon, an imprint of HarperCollins*Publishers* Ltd,
1 London Bridge Street, London, SE1 9GF

www.harpercollins.co.uk

HarperCollins*Publishers*, Macken House, 39/40 Mayor Street Upper, Dublin 1, D01 C9W8, Ireland

To Wed a Devilish Duke © 2025 Christine Merrill

ISBN: 978-0-263-34525-4

07/25

This book contains FSC™ certified paper
and other controlled sources to ensure responsible forest management.

For more information visit www.harpercollins.co.uk/green.

Printed and Bound in the UK using 100% Renewable Electricity
at CPI Group (UK) Ltd, Croydon, CR0 4YY

To Katy and Cory. Solidarity for ever.

Prologue

Julian Parish, Duke of Septon, settled into his usual chair at White's and signalled for a brandy, ignoring the disapproving stares of the men around him and the way they shifted in their chairs as if they could not decide whether to storm out of the room in disgust or lean closer to learn what shocking thing he was likely to do next. He was used to the censure of his fellows and usually gave it no notice. With a reputation such as his, it was hardly a surprise when the old prigs that frequented this place turned up their noses and muttered about the sort of people that the club was accepting nowadays.

But on this morning, he was almost willing to admit that he had gone too far. He glanced at the glass in his hand and wondered if it was too early in the day for strong spirits. Then he drank till it was empty and signalled for another, taking care that his hand did not tremble as he did so. Damn, but he had needed that drink.

It was not every day that one almost killed a man.

He might actually have done so, if not for the quick intervention of the surgeon, who had been bribed to look the other way so that he could not swear to how the injury had happened. Duelling was still illegal, and they were all risking arrest for ignoring the laws and breaking the peace.

The fact that everyone agreed his opponent had deserved it did not matter. Decent men did not go around running other gentlemen through. When faced with the despicable behaviour of another, they simply ignored it and proved that their own morals were suspect.

But Julian could no longer stand by and do nothing. He had promised that he would protect the girl that Westbridge had insulted. And though others might doubt it, his honour still meant something to him. So he had issued a challenge and acted upon it.

And now Westbridge was on the edge of death, and Julian was properly in the soup.

Under the circumstances, a visit to Italy might be in order. Or at least a tour of his lands and estates. Something to take him from London while his opponent recovered and interest in justice waned. But he had never run from a thing in his life and had no desire to start now. Besides, the estates were in perfect order and continental travel was never as grand as one hoped it would be.

He grinned and drank again. The law be damned. He had done what more than a few men had wanted but lacked the nerve to carry out. The Duke of Westbridge was a rake and had earned his punishment.

He ought to know, for he was one himself.

Chapter One

Portia Braddock had always considered herself an unexceptionable young lady. She was pretty enough, if one discounted her slightly uneven smile and her neck, which she felt was a trifle too long. She was smart enough, but not overly so, having little head for languages and none at all for mathematics. She kept current with fashion but did not allow herself to be swayed into wearing unflattering styles just to attract attention.

Her friends were ordinary as well. She did not run with a fast set or court scandal in any way. She had planned, by the end of this Season, to make an unexceptional marriage to an unexceptional man and be moderately content with the life he provided her.

It was rather boring, but she did not think it was likely to change. If in secret, she longed for something more? She had far too much sense to do anything that would make her notorious. Her mother was counting on her to make a match this Season, and she would do nothing to jeopardise the chance to be a proper wife to an equally proper man.

That was why, when her reputation was ruined, it came as such a surprise. She had been home in bed, sound asleep and dreaming unexceptional dreams, when the event occurred that would change her life. It was not until she came down to breakfast and read the scandal sheets that she learned of it, and it took some days to understand the repercussions.

A week later, she was silently praying that things were not as bad as they seemed. But the papers were still posting regular updates on the situation, describing the Duke of W's condition as grim and his assailant, The Duke of S, as unrepentant. Worst of all, the speculations on what Miss B had done to bring the two men to blows grew wilder with each passing day.

She winced as she read the latest article, then walked across the breakfast room to throw the paper into the fire. 'Today it says I am the mistress of Westbridge. Yesterday it was Septon. Tomorrow it will likely be both. What am I to do?'

'You can start by not reading the gossip columns,' her mother said in an even voice. 'There is nothing we can say that will affect what they write, and it only upsets you.'

'But it is so unfair,' she said. 'I have done nothing at all to deserve this.'

But after a week of rumours, even her own mother was looking at her with doubt. 'Are you sure?'

'At the last ball we attended, I spoke to the Duke of Westbridge. But only briefly and in plain sight of dozens of people. We were never unchaperoned. No one remarked on it at the time. I saw him speak to half a dozen young ladies in the same way.'

'How did he behave?'

'He flirted with me. But then, he flirts with everyone. I did not take it seriously, nor did I give him reason to think that there would be anything more than that between us.' Their brief conversation had been a bright spot in a dull evening, for Westbridge was handsome, witty and titled, far more exciting than the men who usually noticed her. If a few words shared at a ball was reason for a duel, the men of London would be fighting continually.

'And the Duke of Septon?' her mother pressed. 'He was the one who issued the challenge.'

'I have not spoken to him at all,' she said, even more baffled. 'Not since Father's funeral, at least. And that was a year and a half ago. At the time, he offered condolences. Nothing more.'

'He was a friend of your father's,' her mother said with a disapproving sniff. 'If one can call such a scoundrel a true friend. I am surprised he bothered to attend the service. I'd made it clear that he was not welcome.'

Portia nodded dutifully. She did not know enough about Septon to have an opinion. If the gossips were to be believed, he was a danger to young ladies, so she kept her distance. But those same rumour-mongers claimed she was a fallen woman, so perhaps there was no truth in their stories.

She'd seen him at several balls and soirées this Season and could not help admiring him, for he was a singularly handsome man. His hair was black, his body lean and graceful and his features sharp. Though he smiled often, the light of it never reached his dark eyes. It made her wonder if he was bored, or just sad. Perhaps the dissipation he was supposed to be steeping in gave him no lasting pleasure. But in all the time she'd spent in covert observation of him, he had never turned that sad gaze on her or made any attempt to speak to her, except for that brief meeting at the graveside.

Why would a man who had shown no interest in her issue a challenge to defend her honour? There was no explanation for the predicament he had landed her in by doing so. Only a fool or a madman would fight to the death over someone he barely knew.

'The papers must be wrong,' she insisted for the

hundredth time. 'I had nothing to do with this matter, whatever they might say. There must have been some other argument between them.'

'We will have a hard time convincing anyone of that, now that the rumours have spread,' her mother said, shaking her head in dismay. 'And I had such hopes for this Season.'

'As had I.' While her father had been alive, it had been possible to ignore their money troubles. He had assured them that any financial problems were temporary and could be fixed by spending one or two nights at a gaming table. Since his death, her mother had been forced to confront the bills he'd hidden from them and the pitifully small settlement they were expected to survive upon. Action had to be taken.

So, they had gambled, not as Father had done, but in a way genteel ladies did when faced with the poorhouse. They had thrown off their mourning clothes and spent money they could not spare on new gowns for the many balls and parties that were a feature of the Season, searching for a man who could afford a wife with modest needs, and if possible, a mother-in-law who would be ever so grateful for his assistance.

And now it had all come to ruin.

'Since the duel, we have not received a single new invitation,' her mother said.

'I have not heard a word from any of the gentlemen

who were eager to walk out with me before,' Portia agreed. 'Not one visit from friends or suitors in almost a week. Not even to express sympathy. It is as if we no longer exist.'

'They are all too aware that we are here,' her mother said in a grim voice. 'They simply do not wish to be seen with us, and it is not likely to change. We must come up with a new plan.'

'But what can we do?' Portia asked. 'I doubt that anyone will hire me as a governess or companion after seeing my name in the papers.'

'Perhaps we should move to the country,' her mother said. 'I could write to my cousins in Shropshire. We could stay with them until the scandal passes.'

'Your cousins are as poor as we are,' Portia reminded her. 'And did not approve of Father. They have made it clear that they do not welcome company.'

'Well, we cannot remain here with things as they are,' her mother said, shaking her head. 'I am afraid that the *ton* has made up its mind about you. Your name is now irrevocably linked to these two unspeakable men. Septon especially, for he was the one to issue the challenge.'

'Perhaps, if I go to him and seek clarification…'

Her mother's denial came before Portia could finish the thought. 'If you go to either of these horrible men and someone hears of it, it will only confirm the suspicions that there is something going on.'

'Then I am to be ruined without any of the advantages involved in falling into sin?' she said, unable to resist a smile.

'Advantages?' her mother said.

'There must be some, mustn't there? The courtesans I've seen when we go to the theatre look to be a happy bunch, as do the opera dancers and actresses on the stage.' She considered. 'Perhaps, now that I am a fallen woman, I could present myself at the Theatre Royale and ask if they have need of performers.'

'Certainly not,' her mother said, horrified.

'Do you expect me to accept a genteel spinsterhood, because two men who are strangers to me had an argument?' she said.

'I do not want that,' her mother assured her. 'But neither do I want you to do something so dishonourable as taking to the stage.'

'Then I shall have to marry,' she said, her eyes sparkling as a plan formed in her mind. 'And I know of two men at least who will not be bothered by my newly tarnished reputation, since they are the ones who destroyed it. If they thought it worth the trouble of arguing over me, they must find me at least a little bit attractive.'

'They are the two biggest rakes in London,' her mother declared. 'I forbid you to go near them.'

'If I am going to make a mistake, it might as well be a big one.'

Her mother shook her head, exasperated. 'Perhaps you do not understand what a rake is, my dear. If they were fighting over you, it can mean nothing good. They are the sort of men that do not marry the women they dishonour.'

'Perhaps that is because no woman has ever asked them to,' Portia said, warming to the idea. Since it was clear that no one was coming to save her, she would have to take the initiative. She would go to these men and ask—no, demand—that they make things right.

Now her mother was looking at her in a way that raised the sort of fears that troubled her late at night, after an evening of dancing with the sort of boring men who had been willing to pay court to her thus far. There was a tinge of pity in that look. As if her mother knew she was nothing special and destined for a dull future. She simply wasn't the sort of girl that things were ever going to happen to.

Then she remembered that this could not possibly be true. Something had already happened to set her apart from the crowd. It was just a matter of finding a way to work it to her advantage.

She gave her mother her bravest smile. 'Septon and

Westbridge are dukes and will have to marry eventually for the succession if nothing else. When they decide to do so, they will be seeking a girl of good character who will not interfere in their debauchery. I could manage that quite well. I like nothing better than sitting at home with a good book. I should probably like it even better if I was doing it in a ducal manor with a full staff.'

Her mother's reaction to this could best be described as horror-struck amazement. 'You don't know what it is to be married to such a man. The heartache that comes with being yoked to a womanising cad. You will never know where he is or who he is with or what he is doing. Septon and Westbridge are no better than your father was.'

And there was the nub of her mother's argument. Father had been a rake, and she had married him with stars in her eyes, only to be bitterly disappointed when marriage did not change him. Fortunately, Portia was not so naive. 'I know you wanted something better for me,' she said gently. 'But it will be different than it was with you and Father.'

'How can you think so? Either one of these men would break your heart just for sport.'

'Not if I do not give it over to them,' she said firmly. 'It is not as if I am doing this for love. A marriage to one of them will be little more than a business transaction. I can be a biddable wife who will provide them with the heirs they need and stay properly out of the way once that need has been filled. Either one of them will have more than enough money to keep me in comfort and take care of you as well.'

Her mother's doubtful expression wavered at the mention of monetary support, so Portia pushed forward, supporting her argument. 'It will be far better for you if I married a rich peer than the gentlemen of modest means who have courted me thus far. All I could have promised with any of them was that I would relieve part of your financial burden by removing myself from your household. But suppose I could promise you a house all your own with servants and space to entertain? Great men like Septon and Westbridge have more properties than they have time to visit. It is not like they will miss the space if you move into one of them.'

'That is probably true,' her mother said. 'But…'

Portia pressed on. 'With mutual disinterest on both sides, we might manage quite successfully as a married couple in modern society. Such a marriage would be better than I'd hoped for under other circumstances. On my best day, I did not think I would land a man with a title. And now I have two of them halfway to the altar.'

The last was an exaggeration. She did not even

know if they would agree to see her, much less consider her offer. But if she was going to do this, she needed all the confidence she could gather. She would not admit defeat before she had tried.

Before she could be interrupted, she went on with her plan. 'The main question, as I see it, is, which one should I choose? Must I flip a coin? Do I throw my sympathies with the winner of the duel or the loser?'

'Choosing a husband at random? That is even more horrible than becoming an actress,' her mother said.

'How else am I to do it?' she asked, honestly curious. After half a Season of husband-hunting, she was beginning to wonder if she had no heart to lose. She had always hoped that, when it came time to marry, she would feel at least a bit of emotion for the man who'd offered. But so far, the men she'd met were all very like one another, interchangeable in their looks, their flattery and their approach to courtship. If more than one of them had offered, she would have closed her eyes and made a wild guess as to the better choice.

So it was with these two strangers. They were both dukes, though Septon was dark and Westbridge fair. They were of similar age, nearly thirty, both handsome and well-educated. If gossip was to be believed, they were equally wicked. They each had London townhouses, large estates, and all the trappings of wealth and rank. If she married either of them, she would have access to privileges she had never imagined. At least not until now.

Then she thought of Septon's sad eyes. He looked like a man who needed company. He had been kind to Father and had come to the funeral to console her in her lowest moment. A man like that could not be all bad.

Not just a man, she reminded herself. A handsome duke. If she was wrong about him, she would at least be in an unassailable social position. 'Being a duchess is never a bad thing,' she said firmly. How could it be?

Her mother was staring at her now with a decidedly dubious expression. 'And what if they refuse you?'

'Then I shall be no worse off than I am now,' she replied. 'But I shall not know until I try.' She considered for a moment. 'I shall start with Septon. Society blames him for this incident, so his reputation is in greatest need of repair. Westbridge is still recovering from his wounds and might not be as receptive to my suggestions, if he is even conscious to receive them at all.' If she was honest, she preferred the first choice. A dark-haired man with a good heart, a tortured soul and eyes that she could not forget.

She put the thought aside as quickly as she had it, for it sounded like the sort of romantic claptrap that she was trying to avoid. The goal of this marriage was to keep her mother from destitution and not to live out the plot of a Minerva novel. 'Septon,' she said with a firm smile and a nod. 'I will visit him immediately and have the matter settled by lunch.'

'If you must go, take a maid with you,' her mother said, with a defeated wave of her hands. 'If these horrible men do not laugh in your face and turn you away, they might attempt to destroy what is left of your reputation. Whatever you do, do not meet with them alone, for they cannot be trusted.'

'Very well,' Portia said with a sigh and went to her room to prepare to meet her hopefully future husband.

It was nearly ten o'clock in the morning, and though many of the *ton* had already breakfasted and were out on Rotten Row for an early ride, Julian was on foot and making his way home. Parliament would not be in session until afternoon, which meant he still had time for a nap and a wash and perhaps something to take the edge off the foul head he had after a night's drinking and gaming. At least the fresh air was clearing the tobacco smoke from his clothing and his brain, so he did not feel as disreputable as he probably looked.

It often occurred to him on these shameful ambles home that the life he was living was not good for his constitution. A few more years of it and the marks of dissipation would be something that could not be napped away. He did not want to end up like poor George Braddock.

Though he had been almost old enough to be Julian's father, Braddock had been excellent company and the truest of friends, and they had passed many an evening drinking, gaming and happily flouting propriety. But he had died at seven and forty, proof that while the spirit might enjoy reckless living, the body could not support it for ever.

It was not that the prospect of death frightened Julian. A part of him would welcome an end to this fruitless life he was living. It was just that he hoped, when it came, it would be quick like the snuffing of a candle and not slow and wasting, leaving him bedbound and full of regrets as George had been.

Some men had thoughts such as this in the dark watches of the night, at three or perhaps four o'clock. But he'd found, if one did not go to bed, one could prevent such worrying until midmorning. With the sun up, it was easier to chase the demons of doubt away.

A footman let him in at the front door of his Mayfair townhouse and, if the servant felt any disdain at his master's poor condition, he did not show it. But Julian expected that there was talk about him below stairs, at least amongst the staff who had been here when his father was alive. Old Septon had been upright and strait-laced to a degree seldom seen in London society. He was a paragon of virtue, an example to all English men of the superiority of the ruling class.

At least he had been so in public. When people were not watching, he had been much different. And, unlike poor Braddock, the old hypocrite had lived long enough to see his heir grow into a complete disappointment. He had called Julian a thorn in his side, a womanising wastrel that would bring infamy to the family and the title.

Julian was all that and proud to be so. But at least he was honest about it. He did not pretend to be something other than he was, as his father had done. He wore his sins for all to see, and society could do what they liked with that. The fact that so few people had the nerve to cut him proved that the *ton* was little more than a sanctimonious mob and unworthy of the wealth and position they'd inherited.

He removed his hat and handed it to Banks, the butler, who was probably disappointed in him as well. He had been there at the door since Julian had been in leading strings and had higher standards than any duke in the realm. While some might fire him for his insolence, Julian took comfort in the man's honesty. With Banks, at least one knew where one stood.

'Good morning, Banks,' he said with a smile that was certain to vex the old retainer.

Banks stared at him and gave the slightest sniff of

disapproval at his rumpled coat, muddy boots and the faint odour of rum that still clung to his breath. Then he looked at his watch as if to verify that it was not yet noon. 'Indeed, Your Grace. It is a very good morning.' He stepped in front of Julian, blocking the way to his bedroom. 'There is a lady to see you. A Miss Braddock,' he added. He seemed faintly pleased at the response to the name, which coursed through Julian like a lightning bolt.

'Portia Braddock?' he said weakly. It had to be. There was no other.

'I believe so,' Banks replied. He remained outwardly impassive, but there was something about the set of his mouth that hinted he was rejoicing at his master's suffering.

'Tell her I am not at home.'

'I have already done so,' the butler replied in a tone that hinted he thought his master was an idiot. 'She insisted she would wait for your return.'

'I cannot meet her like this,' he said, trying to ignore the slight twitch of the butler's upper lip that was as significant a break in decorum as a guffaw of laughter. 'Tell her I will be down directly.' Then he hurried to his rooms and rang for his valet, pacing before the cheval glass as he surveyed the damage. Did he need a change of linen? A fresh shave?

Such thoughts were ridiculous. A visit from a

woman he barely knew and that was both unexpected and uninvited deserved no special preparation. He should let her see him just as he was, a wreck and a ruin and in no mood for company.

But his vanity would not allow that. If she insisted on seeing him, he wanted to look well, for this, their first and possibly only private meeting.

He was making this call into something more important than it probably was. But he could not help himself. Though they were strangers, he had been watching her for a year and a half. Watching over her, more like. He had not spoken to her or been in close proximity, but even so, she occupied a permanent corner of his mind, a perpetual irritation like a stone in his shoe.

Normally, it was easy to resolve attraction to a beautiful woman. One simply had to bed her and move on. But Miss Braddock was gently born and innocent, and thus beyond his reach. So, what should have been an academic interest in her had become something more like an obsession. She was untouchable, which made him want her all the more.

He had taken no action on it until recently. But the one he'd taken had been extreme and uncalled for. One was not supposed to take up arms with a friend over what had probably been idle conversation about a girl neither of them were courting. But that night, his control had snapped and he had acted like a jealous fool.

Now he was to answer for it, he supposed. She must have heard of the reason for the duel and wanted an explanation. He had very little to give her, other than an embarrassed shrug.

So he allowed his valet to repair some of the damage of his night out before going down to meet her. When he arrived in the receiving room, he was freshly shaved and in a clean shirt and coat. All traces of the evening had been disguised as was his apprehension in seeing her appear in his home with no warning.

He paused in the doorway, allowing himself to look at her, if only for a moment. She was as sweet as she had been when he'd first seen her at her father's funeral. At that time, she had seemed lost in grief, hardly aware of the weak platitudes he had offered her. She was every bit as lovely as George had claimed, and her devotion to him proved that it was possible for children to respect their fathers, no matter how wayward those men might have been.

Time had healed her grief, he hoped. She had cast off her mourning clothes some six months ago, and today she was smartly dressed in blue linen, her dark blonde curls sprouting from under a fashionable bonnet. And, as she had at the funeral, she was staring at him with the largest hazel eyes he'd ever seen.

He allowed himself to stare back into those eyes for a moment, letting the light in them soothe his spirit. There was a quiet intelligence there, a beauty that would not dim with time. He could gaze into those eyes for ever and never grow tired of them.

And he would be an idiot for doing so. Just as he'd been when he'd picked a fight with Westbridge. Look what trouble that had caused.

He broke the gaze and looked to the other woman sitting in the corner of the room. Miss Braddock had had the good sense to bring a maid with her. It pleased him, for he had always imagined her to be a sensible girl. As an added precaution, he left the door to the room open, so his servants could be certain that there would be nothing untoward in this unconventional meeting.

'Miss Braddock,' he said, with a bow. 'To what do I owe this honour?'

'I might ask you the same question, Your Grace,' she said, with no preamble. 'The papers say that you and Westbridge have been fighting over me. I want to know why.'

The question was not unexpected, but it came so suddenly that it left him lost for words. He swallowed to buy time, struggling to regain his composure, hoping that his explanation would have none of the pent-up emotion that had driven him to act so unwisely in the first place. 'We had both been drinking.'

'I am sure that is true of many nights,' she replied, giving him a searching look. 'And none of those resulted in a duel. What happened this time?'

'He said something that I took exception to,' he admitted.

'And what might that have been?' she prodded.

'Something that is not for a lady's ears,' he said, hoping that would be enough.

'Perhaps a paraphrase would be helpful,' she said, offering no quarter. Her maid leaned forward, also eager to hear.

He swallowed again, unable to hide his discomfort, and searched for the words that would explain. 'He suggested that you might be ripe for seduction.'

'Ripe,' she said, her perfect lips tasting the word in a way that made him wonder if his former friend had been right all along. 'As if women are nothing more than fruit to be picked and tasted.'

'Exactly,' he said, relieved that she understood.

'Are gentlemen in the habit of making such statements, when ladies are not present?' she said, her golden eyes wide with curiosity.

'Not if they are truly gentlemen,' he said awkwardly.

Miss Braddock did not seem shocked by this, so

much as curious. 'And Westbridge is not truly a gentleman?' she asked, still staring at him.

'He was not behaving as such,' he responded, feeling a sudden flare of anger that was still unquenched, even after the duel.

'And you,' she said, with a searching look that made him even more uncomfortable. 'Are you a gentleman?'

It would be a lie to say he was any better than Westbridge had been. 'If you have to ask, then you already know the answer,' he said. He was aware of his reputation and had never been ashamed of it. At least, not until today.

'Why did you choose that moment to stand on honour? You hardly know me.' She gave him another probing look and waited in silence for his answer.

He had no choice but to confess the truth. Part of it, at least. He doubted she would be happy about it, for who liked having their lives arranged for them by others? 'I made a promise to your father to look after you,' he said, looking away.

'You visited him in his last days,' she said with a nod, then looked at him expectantly, waiting for further explanation.

'He was worried about your future,' he said, feeling as awkward and foolish as he had on the day he'd made the vow. 'That some man might take advantage of you when he was not there to protect you. He wanted you to be safe and marry well.'

'He set you to watch over me.' Her expression changed to one of scepticism. 'You?'

He could not blame her for doubting the wisdom of the choice. At the time, he'd not believed it either.

'Why me?' he'd asked, and the other man had laughed.

'Set a thief to catch a thief,' Braddock had replied in a hoarse voice. *'Who better to protect my little girl from predatory men than one who knows all their tricks?'*

'He said I was his closest friend,' he said with a shrug. And though Braddock was older by nearly twenty years, Julian had felt the same. George had understood him far better than old Septon had and never wasted time in judgement or recrimination. 'In some ways, he was like a father to me,' he said, thinking back to the time they had spent together.

'Which would make you like a brother to me,' she said, even more sceptically.

When he looked at her, he did not feel in any way fraternal. Still, he jumped on the analogy, which put a better face on what had happened. 'You had no male relatives to take your future in hand. So, he tasked me to keep an eye on you.'

'You have not made much of a job of it,' she replied. 'You have said nothing about it until this moment.'

'Because you did not need much watching,' he replied. 'You have done nothing that worried me, and the gentlemen showing interest in you are respectable enough. Not a fortune hunter in the bunch.'

'If they wished to hunt fortunes, they would be fools to chase after me,' she said, rolling her eyes. She looked at him again. 'Why did you think Westbridge was a threat to me? He had done nothing as of yet, to harm me.'

Why, indeed? He should have let the man's comment pass as idle talk. But something about it had rankled. He had emptied his glass and demanded that the fellow take back what he'd said, but Westbridge had only laughed.

So he had slapped him and issued a challenge.

He was not sure, even now, if that was what George Braddock had wanted from him when he'd made him swear to protect Portia. But it had been the only thing he could think of at the time.

The girl was still staring at him, her bright, inquisitive eyes making him uneasy. They saw too much, he was sure, reading beneath the surface of his words, searching for truths he did not want to reveal. If he wasn't careful, she would realise that the promise he'd made to her father had eaten into him, like a worm in an apple, until he could not stop thinking about her, wondering what would become of her now that she was old enough to marry. And to imagine what it might be like if he had been a better man, the sort who could be worthy of her.

It was a ridiculous idea, almost as foolish as the duel had been. But he refused to admit he was wrong to fight Westbridge, to her or anyone else. He was not in the habit of apologising for his actions and did not mean to start now. 'Perhaps he meant no harm. Or, perhaps he did. In either case, I left him in no condition to bother you and have taught him to mind his tongue in the future.'

She stared at him a moment longer, and when it was clear that he had no more answer to give her, she sighed. 'Well, you have made a fine mess of things by your actions. The *ton* thinks I am somehow to blame for it all and deserving of punishment.'

'You did nothing,' he assured her. Nothing she could control, at least. For what could be done about the attentions of men such as himself and his former friend? She was beautiful. Men would look at her and think what they would. The day gown she was wearing was in no way revealing, but he had an exceptionally good imagination and could picture the full breasts and trim waist hidden beneath it and silently agreed with Westbridge. She was ripe as a summer peach.

And such a reaction to an innocent young woman said more about him and his lack of morals than it did about her. But he could not think of a thing to do that would make the gossip any less, now that it had begun. 'Time will change the tide of opinion,' he said at last. 'As long as no one gets wind of this visit you have paid me.' He gave her maid a direct look, and the girl gave a nod of agreement. 'There is little else I can do but encourage you to be patient and ignore the gossips. That is what I mean to do.' Then he stepped to the side to give her and her maidservant a clear path to the door and hoped they would take the hint and depart.

'I do not have time,' she said, her brow furrowing. 'I am twenty-two years old, and as you have established, I am ripe now. I will stale just as quickly. My come out was delayed because of Father's illness and death. There was hardly enough money for this Season and there's none left for a second. In the year or so it will take for the gossip to die down, I will be well on the way to wallflower status. It is a short hop from there to spinster.' She clasped her hands in her lap for they had begun to flutter nervously.

He stared at them, long-fingered, graceful. He could imagine them touching him, the feather-light strokes across his bare skin meant to tease and arouse. He cleared his throat and forced himself to focus on her face. 'Surely you exaggerate.'

'Suppose I do not?' she replied. 'Young ladies do not have the advantages that gentlemen do, to pick and choose what their futures might be. If you knew my father, then you must realise he was a gambler, and not very lucky, at that. He left us with very little. I have naught to hope for but a good marriage to a man generous enough to care for myself and my mother. We have nothing between us but debts.' She gave him another, considering look. 'And, apparently, you, as a protector.' She stared at him, waiting.

'If you wish me to provide for you both, I can afford to do so,' he said. 'But I do not think that is wise. If anyone were to find out, they would think even worse of you than they do now.'

'Or you can simply marry me,' she said.

The statement was so ridiculous that for a moment, he was not sure he'd heard it correctly. Then the words registered, and he laughed.

But she did not join him, only stared at him with that same expectant look she had worn since she had entered the room.

He sobered. 'You are serious?'

The stare continued, direct and disconcerting.

'You can't be,' he said, feeling rising alarm.

'Very,' she said flatly. 'You and Westbridge are the

only two men in London who know for certain that I have done nothing to earn the horrible things that are being said about me in the papers. You, particularly, must know of my good character, if you have been watching me these last months. And Westbridge must find me attractive, if he was foolish enough to speculate about me.'

'Do not bring Westbridge into this,' he said, taking an involuntary step towards her.

Her eyes narrowed ever so slightly, as if she had spotted a weakness in him. Then she said, 'I have come to you first because, according to the scandal sheets, you are the one who is still capable of speech.'

At this blunt reminder of what he'd done, he winced. 'I heard Westbridge is recovering.'

'The papers seem to think so,' she agreed. 'But as of yet, they say he is seeing no visitors.'

'But when he does, you will go to him?' Something stirred in him at the thought. The same dark thing that had caused him to take up a sword in the first place.

She gave him a curious smile. 'Is there a reason I should not ask him?'

'Because he is a rake,' Julian said.

'So are you.'

'He got what he deserved,' Julian insisted, unable to help himself.

The curiosity in her eyes seemed to intensify, focusing on him like a sunbeam. 'What he said might have passed unnoticed, but your response to it ruined my chances of making a match.'

'I do not think…' he began.

'Did not think, more likely,' she cut in.

'It was a rash act,' he admitted.

Her eyebrows rose.

'I sometimes act before thinking,' he muttered. Her tarnished reputation was not his fault, and he refused to apologise for the rumours started by the sanctimonious gossips of the *ton*.

She continued to gaze at him.

'I had to do something,' he declared. 'There are rules of decorum…'

'Which you frequently bend with impunity,' she reminded him. 'The law against duelling, for example. If you had kept that rule and ignored his comment, it would have gone no further, and my reputation would have been safe.'

That was probably true. If they'd spoken about any other woman, it would not have angered him so. But he had felt responsible for Portia, and the thought of her with Westbridge had driven him near to madness. 'Your father should never have trusted me with your care. You'd have been better off without my help.'

'I do not disagree,' she said quietly, making him feel even worse than he already did. 'The question is, what are you prepared to do about the damage you have done to me?' The look she gave him pierced his carefully curated façade of ennui and struck right to the core of his being.

'Do?' The single word was all he could manage for it felt like all the air had been sucked from the room, leaving him light-headed. Or perhaps it was just the thought of her as his wife, in his arms, at his disposal that made his head spin.

'You know what I want,' she reminded him.

'You do not think that I...' he began, his heart beating in a frantic way that would be most embarrassing, should anyone hear it.

'If you won't have me, then I will go to Westbridge,' she stated with none of the passion he was feeling. 'Unless you can think of some other man who would have me, with no dowry and a ruined reputation.'

'You cannot marry Westbridge,' he said automatically. 'Or me,' he added, embarrassed to admit the truth.

'Whyever not?'

'We are...not the sort of men that a lady like you deserves.' Sanity was returning as he remembered the gap that stood between them. He had done things that had put him far outside the reach of decent society and the ladies that inhabited it. But when he looked at Portia Braddock, he felt a stirring in his soul, or perhaps it was merely in his loins. He had fought for her because, against all logic, he wanted her and could not bear the thought that Westbridge did as well.

'Nonsense,' she said in a cool voice. 'When you marry, as you must, you will put aside your scruples and choose a decently bred young lady, not one you have already ruined.'

'That is not...' But it was true. He did not think of marriage often, but practically speaking, he would be expected to find some milk-and-water virgin and settle down eventually. If he waited much longer, he would be an aging roue, an object of even greater pity than the young wife he chose.

He shuddered at the thought.

But as he looked at Portia Braddock, he felt desire knotting in him, but with none of the guiltless pleasure he usually felt. She was so good, so innocent. It would be wrong.

And yet, just as wrong to walk away from the damage he'd done to her.

'You have done me a great wrong,' she reiterated. 'Making me a duchess would balance the scales quite nicely, I think.'

'You want me for my title?' he said, and the confusion in him hardened into bitterness, which was much easier to understand.

'Not you specifically,' she corrected. 'Either you or

Westbridge could give me what I want. It would be the match of the Season if I were to marry a duke, especially one that had made such a show of avoiding the altar. People who scorn me now would be forced to scrape and bow and give me respect that they never would have, had I married some nobody.'

His eyes narrowed as he looked at her, searching for the mercenary glint in her eye that matched those words. But her expression remained as clear and pure as it had been since he'd first seen her. The appealing innocence that attracted him to her was nothing more than a clever disguise, hiding a heart as hard as a flint.

She continued. 'For either of you, I could be an ideal wife. I would provide you with children and manage your household. I would not question how you spent your time. You could be every bit as wicked as you are now and not give me a second thought. Best of all, the trouble you created for yourself by duelling Westbridge would disappear.' She gave an airy wave of her hand. 'People would think it a love match and call your defence of me romantic.'

The desire that he felt for her was blending with resignation. At the funeral, he had seen a lost girl in need of protection, and it touched his heart. It seemed appearances were deceiving. 'In reality, we would not care for each other at all,' he reminded her, surprised to feel a tightness in his chest at the prospect of such an empty union.

'Did you really expect to marry for love?' she said, giving him another curious glance. 'I had no such plans for this Season. I meant to take whatever offer I received and be grateful for it.' Then her expression hardened. 'It was a modest dream, but now it is quite unattainable. London expects me to run for the country and live in poverty as a spinster with a tainted past. But I would much rather be a duchess and watch all who have gossiped about me eat their words.'

And there it was. The thing he had always suspected about the young ladies of the *ton* but had not wanted to face. They were a mercenary bunch, as selfish in their own way as he was in his. The cold-blooded calculation hidden in those questing hazel eyes made him want to punish her for her arrogance. It would serve her right to be bound for life to the sort of man he took pleasure in being, incapable of tender emotion.

'You say you would not care about my behaviour. You would not question my comings or goings?' he said with a sceptical laugh, hoping that she would retract her words.

'Would it do any good?' she asked.

'Probably not,' he admitted. He had sometimes imagined that the love of a good woman would give him reason to change his ways. But love was not what he felt when he looked at her. How could it be? He did not know her.

What he felt was nothing more than lust. Once she was no longer forbidden fruit, this fever he felt when he looked at her would burn away. It was her inexperience that attracted him. And that was something that would not last an hour, much less a whole night, once they were alone.

But good God, what an hour that would be.

He took a step towards her.

In the corner, the maid shifted and cleared her throat to remind him they were not alone.

'I am intrigued,' he admitted.

'I am glad to hear it,' she replied sedately.

'And we need not love each other at all,' he repeated. 'There will be no nonsense. No tears. No fighting over my drinking, my gambling, my whoring?'

At this last she blinked, and for a moment, he thought he saw fear in her. But it disappeared as quickly as it had come, replaced by resolve. 'It would not be my place to do so,' she said.

'I promised your father I would take care of you,' he said, wondering what George would have thought of such a union. He'd likely have been horrified. But really, what better could he do for her than give her the protection of his name? 'I must think on this. Marriage is a sacrament, after all, and not to be entered into lightly.'

He was joking, but she did not laugh. Instead, she nodded. 'You may have a day. If I have not heard from you by tomorrow at noon, I will go to Westbridge.' She rose and the maid did as well, falling in behind her like a shadow. 'Good day, Your Grace.'

'And to you, Miss Braddock,' he said, turning to catch a whiff of her perfume as she walked past him and out his front door.

Chapter Two

As they made their way home in the rented carriage, Portia slumped in her seat, exhausted. Talking to Septon had been like playing chess with a master. It had required nerves of steel and all her concentration to counter his moves without losing her pieces. In the end, they had played to a draw. 'That went well,' she said to no one in particular.

'If you say so, Miss,' the maid, Rose said, doubt plain in her voice.

'He could have turned me out without allowing me to speak,' she said, thinking aloud. 'Instead, he is at least willing to entertain the idea.' She touched her temple, surprised to feel her hand shaking against her clammy skin. 'I hope he agrees, for I do not think I have the nerve to do this again with another rake.' She smiled weakly and pulled herself up to sit straight. 'But it will not come to that. I think I put my argument quite sensibly. I laid out the advantages to both sides, and I did my best not to sound like some silly girl who wanted to be romanced and doted on. He would not want that, I think.'

'I wouldn't know,' Rose replied, a little too honestly.

'I hope I did not seem too cold,' Portia added, hoping for a reassurance that did not come. 'Perhaps I should have stressed that it would be an honour to take his name. He must be aware that he is sought after, even though his reputation is not what it could be. Most girls would give their eyeteeth to make such a match. I would never have presumed, of course. If it had not been for the circumstances…'

She'd had only to look at him to realise that he was far out of her reach. He had been magnificent, leaning against the door-frame, his long legs crossed at the ankle, his head cocked a little to one side as he listened to her, relaxed and unfazed by her outrageous suggestion. She wondered if he had been so dispassionate when he'd fought Westbridge. What would it take to put him out of composure? Nothing her exceptionally ordinary mind could imagine.

That was the problem with this scheme. She had been hoping for an uncomplicated marriage to an equally uncomplicated man. But Septon was a puzzle, and she did not think she had the wits to solve even a small part of him. As he had ushered her to the door, he had smiled at her. And she'd thought—

no, she was sure—that his smile had changed from the one he'd given her when he had first greeted her. There had been something in it, a message to her that she could not read.

Looking at him then, she'd felt a weakening in her knees and her resolve. She'd wanted to send the maid away so they might be alone, if only for a few minutes, so she could discover what it was he was thinking when he looked at her in that knowing, possessive way.

Perhaps that was what her mother had meant when she'd warned that the man was dangerous. 'Perhaps I should not have done this,' she blurted, looking to Rose again.

'You will forgive me for asking, Miss,' Rose said softly. 'But if just talking to the man for a few minutes leaves you in such a state, how will you ever manage to be his wife?'

How indeed? 'Maybe it will not be so bad,' she said, trying to convince herself. 'He will not be around much, I suspect. What reason would he have to be so, if I am nothing to him?'

'There is one that I can think of,' the maid said in a significant tone.

'And what is that?' Portia said, honestly curious.

'Has your mother not explained to you what marriage entails?' the maid said with a worried shake of her head.

'What is there to explain?' Portia asked. 'I have been well trained in the running of a household. There will be children. But a duke can afford nannies and governesses, so that will not all fall to me.'

'Children,' the maid said, with another dubious look.

'We shall have those, of course,' she said. 'That is the whole point of him marrying, is it not?'

'You will have to be together for that to happen,' Rose said.

'I suppose we shall,' she said, trying to show more confidence than she felt on the subject.

'And do you know what happens, when a man and a woman are alone?'

By the way Rose was looking at her, she was missing some important details. 'Mother said I did not need to know such things until my wedding night and that my husband would teach me all.' The murky explanation had not worried her until now, for if most women managed to produce, how difficult could it be? 'Circumstances would be the same with any man I married, would they not?'

'The Duke of Septon is not just any man,' Rose said with a sigh of exasperation and something else that looked like envy.

Rose was probably right. Her heart did not normally race when she spoke to other gentlemen, as it had when she talked to Septon. Perhaps it was because she had never talked to a duke before.

Or perhaps it was something more. He was very tall, several inches over six feet. He'd seemed to tower over her even as he leaned against the wall, making no effort to come close. And there was something about the way he looked at her, as if he knew things that she did not...

He probably did. If she was honest, many people knew more than she did about life. Even her maid seemed to have a better understanding of marriage. And both maid and mother seemed to think Septon was beyond her capabilities, as if he was an unbroken stallion and she a novice rider. What was she to do if they were right?

'Perhaps it would be best to ask your mother to explain in more detail, before things go any further,' Rose said gently.

'I will do that,' Portia said.

But when they arrived home and she did, her mother was in no mood to educate her. 'Are you back from your fool's errand?' she said, staring at Portia with hands on hips.

'I spoke to Septon,' she said, forcing herself to return a smile.

'And he refused you,' her mother said.

'Not exactly,' she replied. 'I gave him a day to decide.'

At this, her mother laughed. 'And what will you do tomorrow if he turns you down?'

'Go to Westbridge,' she said, trying not to sound defeated.

Her mother sighed. 'I will make arrangements for us to go to the country,' she said. 'I have not yet written to my aunt in Lincoln. If she will have us, we can be gone by week's end. If you are still not married by next year, perhaps we can return to London.'

'Not until I have talked to both of them,' she insisted. Though her mother was trying to put a brave face on it, Portia was sure that once they left for the country they would never return to London. She could not imagine spending her life as a burdensome poor relation. 'Give me a few days, at least.'

'It will take at least that long to hear back from your aunt,' she said, with a sad shake of her head. 'I will wait, a day or two, until you hear from Septon. But understand, I want the best for you. There is nothing ahead but misery if either of these men agree to your wild scheme. It is not in their nature to care about others, especially not for the women they marry.'

'Perhaps that is why I think they will suit me,' she said, wishing there were a way to explain that would not be hurtful. 'You married for love, Mother, did you not?'

The older woman's face changed at the question. Her eyes grew misty and her mouth softened into a smile. 'It was long ago, and we were both very young. But yes, we were very much in love.'

And what good did it do you?

It was the one question that she never dared ask. By the time she was old enough to understand her parents' union, she could see no sign of that tender emotion, only tears and shouting. But she refused to cause more pain by calling attention to the fact. Instead, she said, as gently as she could, 'I think, not all of us are so fortunate as to experience that particular emotion.'

It was a lie, but a small one. Her mother had grieved for her lost love when Father was alive, and that grief had only intensified after he'd drunk himself to death. If this was what it meant to love, then she'd just as soon do without it.

'If the man is kind, love might grow with time,' her mother said. 'Mutual respect is important as well. Your father was handsome and charming and everything I thought I wanted. But much as he wished to love me, he was incapable of putting our needs before his own pleasure.'

'Septon has a lot more money than Father had,'

Portia said, firmly. 'It will not solve all our problems, but it will certainly buy us a better class of misery.'

'I do not want to see you miserable at all,' her mother said, ignoring the jest. 'I want you to be happy in your marriage. If you wait, in time you will find the right man and all will be well.'

'We have no way of knowing if that will ever happen,' Portia said, giving her a firm smile. 'I have waited long enough for someone to bring me happiness. It is time that I find it for myself. Let us wait to see how Septon responds. If he refuses, perhaps I shall let you take me to the country. But we can worry about that tomorrow.'

'Keep your left up, Your Grace.'

Julian raised his fist, a moment too late. His opponent's punch connected, rocking his head back and opening a trickle of blood from his nose. He wiped it away with his other hand and adjusted his stance to block another attack, then jabbed at the other man's midsection.

It was barely breakfast time, but Julian was already at Gentleman Jackson's emporium for a few rounds of vigorous exercise to start the day. After the night he'd had, he needed something to burn off the fire in his blood and chase away the lurid dreams of Portia Braddock.

She had haunted his sleep, a symphony of curves and soft flesh, her lips parted in invitation, eyes wide with surprise as he told her what he wished to do to her.

And he wished so many things when he looked at her, it felt unseemly, even to his jaded palate. That was probably the trouble. He had done anything he pleased over the years, denying himself no pleasure. Now, when presented with a thing he should not have, he had allowed thoughts of it to consume him.

Until yesterday, Portia Braddock had been the epitome of unattainability. One thing he had never done was break his promise to a friend, certainly not one as good as George Braddock had been. As the man had lain dying, he'd sworn that he would protect Portia, and that no harm would come to her until she was properly married and someone else's responsibility.

Until she had come to him with her mad suggestion, he'd had no trouble with that. He had wanted her, of course. She was a beauty, and he was not blind to the fact. But he had not acted upon his desires. Staying far away from her had gone a good way towards securing her safety, since he was exactly the sort of risk she should be avoiding.

In this, her first Season, he'd made a quiet note of the men who courted her and had found them all to be the sort of fellows he'd thought George would have sought for his only child. They were a boring bunch. Not what he'd consider good company. But also not the kind of men who would lure the lovely Miss Braddock out into the moonlight to take liberties. He knew, because he'd spied on them and there had been nothing to see.

Nothing, that is, but a girl in the blossom of womanhood, with hair and eyes so gold that they might have been made of honey. The sight of her made his mouth water. Her trim body clad in modest gowns, graceful neck bare of jewellery...

A left caught him in the ribs as if punishing him for the direction of his thoughts and he groaned, adjusted his stance and jabbed back before his mind wandered again.

He usually paid no attention to the annual crop of virgins that came to London for the Season, looking like nothing so much as a flock of sheep in their white muslin gowns, just as silly and easily startled. If he was in the mood for seduction, he preferred a woman not a girl, someone who knew how to take and give pleasure.

But when he looked at Portia Braddock, he felt different. He wanted to trace those curves and circle that neck with love bites. He wanted to kiss her until she swooned and then carry her unresisting to his rooms. There he would replace the innocence in those wide eyes with all the forbidden knowledge he'd accumulated. He wanted to pour himself into her, to mark her, to ruin her for all other men.

His sparring partner landed yet another punch, this one to his gut. The force of it left him doubled over and gasping.

'Are you all right, Your Grace?' The other man stepped back, dropping his guard.

Julian held up a hand to assure him, struggling for breath. 'Perhaps that is enough for the day,' he wheezed. 'I am too distracted.'

'As you wish.' The boxing master helped him to a chair and handed him a towel to mop the sweat from his brow.

He wiped his face, wishing he could clear the fantasies from his mind as easily. Since the day he had promised Braddock that he would keep his daughter safe from seduction, he had not been able to stop imagining such a fate for her, in graphic detail.

He had never expected that she would come to him, offering herself in exchange for the protection of his name, as cold and passionless as the worst title hunter the *ton* had to offer. If he didn't have an answer for her by noon today, she would go to Westbridge with the same ludicrous suggestion. Suppose he refused her, only to see her fall into the hands of the very man he'd tried to protect her from?

'Damn you, George,' he muttered under his breath. He could not imagine his friend had wanted such a future for his only child. He'd not wanted her to suffer, like her mother had, with an unfaithful rogue for a husband. Though he had regretted the pain he'd inflicted on his long-suffering wife, George had felt that philandering, drinking and gambling were all much the same, vices that were beyond his control. Stop while you still can, he had warned Julian near the end.

But for me, it was always one more drink, one more woman, one more game. And now it is too late.

Julian had ignored the warning, but at least he'd had the sense not to marry. George's wife had been love-struck and starry-eyed when he'd married her, and he'd proved a bitter disappointment to her. Apparently, between them they'd bred a steel-willed opportunist. Though he had done his best to live up to George's request and keep Portia safe from outside influences, it was hardly his fault if the girl was intent on giving herself to a man of good birth but no character simply so she could lord his title over her friends.

She'd made it quite plain, during her visit, that she did not care at all for the faithful husband her father had hoped she would find. Nor did she care for love, which he'd assumed even the most callous young girl secretly pined for. No, she just wanted the power to pay back her detractors.

When he'd agreed to watch over her, he'd thought Portia Braddock a fine young woman, as sweet and good-hearted as George had claimed her to be. But it seemed this was only the bragging of a fond father about his only child. In his own mind, Julian had built her into something more, the pinnacle of the fair sex, a creature so beautiful and noble that he was unworthy to touch the hem of her gown.

They had both been wrong. She was beautiful as a Greek statue and just as heartless. If he agreed to her plan and made her a duchess, she would be much as his own mother had been: aloof and incapable of love, obsessed with society and her place in it. But where his mother had been quick to remind him that he was a continual disappointment that would never live up to his father, his future wife was clearly well aware of his character and didn't seem to care.

In some ways, that made the fair Miss Braddock even worse. Perhaps she deserved to be shown what life would be like when her husband took pleasure in dragging them both through the mud.

Julian allowed himself a grim smile. It was about time he saw to the matter of continuing the family name. At least he could guarantee the girl's innocence for he'd been watching out for that, himself. That would be gone on the first night of their marriage, as would his obsessive desire for her. In exchange she would have wealth and position beyond anything Braddock had imagined. What better way to discharge his duty to her than by making her his duchess? While he was not the ideal husband, he was the one she probably deserved.

Chapter Three

The next day, Portia stared at the clock in the morning room, counting the ticks and tocks as the hands moved closer to noon. There was only one minute left until her deadline expired, but she had given up on Septon at least half an hour before. If he was coming at all, he'd have been here by now. She must accept the fact that he did not want her.

After luncheon, she would go to Westbridge. Not that she really wanted to. Before meeting Septon, it had been easy to convince herself that all men were the same and that she could marry the one who was most agreeable to it. But it had been harder than she'd expected to look into those very dark eyes and make her offer. As he'd looked at her, she'd felt strangely vulnerable, as if he was looking through her, leaving her no secrets.

He, on the other hand, was completely opaque. Perhaps her mother was right, and she would be better to marry a country gentleman with a spotless reputation. Her life would be dull, but at least she would feel better than she did now. Her nerves were stretched to the breaking point, waiting for an answer that might never come. The point in going to him had been to find a man she did not care about. How had he managed to thwart her by doing nothing at all?

She glanced in the mirror above the fireplace and looked away again. What had she been thinking? Septon could have any girl he wanted. When he chose a bride, he would either pick a great beauty or the daughter of another peer. She was not exceptional in looks or rank and he'd never have noticed her at all if it hadn't been for her father's request. Because of the stupid duel, she had deluded herself into thinking he was interested in her, but he had issued the challenge out of a misplaced sense of duty. Nothing more.

And Westbridge had been talking of seducing her, not marriage. She could not help a little shudder at the thought of having to ask for his help. Perhaps her mother had been right, all along.

Then, just as the clock began to strike twelve, there was a knock on the front door. A moment later, the Duke of Septon was shown into the room. Her mother followed close on his heels to chaperone the meeting, taking a seat on the divan and gesturing their guest to a chair.

Portia watched in fascination as he crossed the room and sat. When she'd surprised him at home, he had seemed almost casual in manner and dress. But today, he was every bit a duke in a coat of deep bottle-green. It was simply cut but exquisitely tailored to display his broad shoulders, trim waist and muscular arms. His buff breeches were similarly well made, accentuating the strength and length of his limbs. His clothes did not so much scream wealth as whisper it. He did not bother with brass buttons or jewelled stickpins. The simple, masculine symmetry of his body was enough.

She knew that it was rude to stare, but there was something about the way he moved, a kind of effortless grace that made it impossible for her to look away. It came with being a peer, she supposed, this innate superiority. Even if he'd come to her dressed in rags, she would have known him for a man with the money and power to change her life.

'Your Grace,' her mother said with a smile that did not reach her eyes. 'It is so kind of you to visit after all this time. It has been a year and a half since the funeral, and we have seen nothing of you.'

Portia shot her a warning look, for the greeting was very near to an insult. She had been rude to him at the funeral as well. It was no wonder that he'd not reached out to them since.

Septon made no answer but bowed to greet them.

He waited as Portia took a seat by the window, then sat as well.

'I did not think you would come,' Portia said, speaking the truth and immediately regretting it.

'Your deadline was noon, was it not?' he said, glancing at the clock, then back at her with a cool smile.

'Or before,' she said tightly.

Their gazes locked, and she felt the same shock of connection they'd shared as he'd smiled at her the day before. How had she ever thought him melancholy? There was no sadness in the depths of the brown eyes that were staring at her now, only heat. The intensity of that stare raised an answering warmth in her that she had sworn she would never feel for him.

Of course, she had also said she would not care about his comings and goings. And just a day after that promise, she was already complaining about his late arrival. He had probably put off this meeting until the literal last minute as a message that he would not be dictated to.

If he was testing her, she had failed.

'The important thing is that you have come,' her mother said, breaking the tension between them. 'Is there something you wished to say to my daughter?'

'Only that I have considered her offer,' he said, still staring at her. 'I am willing to accept on the following terms.' He held up one finger. 'We will be married by special licence.' Another finger. 'The wedding will take place at my home.' Another finger. 'The vicar will refrain from sermonising about the sanctity of the occasion and our duties as husband and wife. We will not be pretending that this is anything more than it is—a mutually beneficial agreement, which will be all but over once we have produced the one or two offspring necessary to secure the succession.'

Her mother released an outraged gasp and prepared to speak, but Portia held up a hand to silence her. 'I have terms as well.'

He laughed. 'You stated the conditions when you came to me yesterday. Do not tell me you have changed your mind.'

She shook her head and gave him what she hoped was a disarming smile. 'Not on anything significant.' She held up a finger of her own. 'I wish there to be an announcement in *The Times*, so that society understands we are wed.' Another finger. 'A small wedding breakfast, after the ceremony. Nothing too elaborate or public. We might hold it in your dining room, if that is convenient.' Another finger. 'And finally, the assurance that you will leave the rearing of the children to me and that I will be a part of their lives, until they are of age. There will be no calling for a divorce and cutting me off from them after they are born. Once we are wed, we will remain so even if it is in name only.'

'Until death us do part,' he said with a nod.

'You agree?' she said, unable to look away from those bottomless eyes.

Say yes.

She willed the words to him, praying for the answer she longed to hear. When he looked at her, as he was doing now, she could not imagine offering herself to Westbridge. It was as if Septon had looked into her soul and stole some vital part of it, leaving her helpless, unwilling to escape.

After an unbearably long silence he replied, 'I agree.' He rose and stepped across the room to take her hand. He clasped it for only a moment, then reached into his coat pocket, fishing around for a moment before producing a ring and slipping it onto her finger. 'The Septon betrothal ring.'

She stared down at the large opal, set in gold, turning her hand and watching the flashes in its milky depths. The stone was considered unlucky by some, since the flame could die and with it, whatever it represented. She hoped it was not a sign of things to come. She looked up at him again and forced herself to smile as if his gesture was a mere formality and not something she would treasure for the rest of her life. 'Thank you. It is lovely.'

He withdrew his hand and offered a brief bow. 'I will be going now, to arrange for the licence and announcement. You will be notified when things have been settled and a date has been set. Submit your breakfast menu to my staff along with the names of any guests you wish to invite.'

'Very well,' she said. 'Good day, Your Grace.'

'And to you, Miss Braddock,' he said. And then he was gone.

Once the front door had closed, her mother erupted with a wordless expression of rage. She sputtered for a moment, like a tea-kettle releasing steam and then said, 'You cannot mean to go through with it.'

Portia released a slow sigh of her own, feeling the tension she'd been holding inside seep away. 'I do. It is all agreed upon.'

'His conditions are just the sort I would expect from a man who puts no value on the union,' her mother said bitterly, shaking her head. 'No banns? No church wedding?'

'If he is as wicked as everyone thinks, he would probably burst into flames on the threshold of St George's,' Portia said, unable to resist a smile.

'That is nothing to joke about,' her mother said, sputtering again.

She rose and went to her mother, taking her hands. 'It is far better to laugh about it than to cry. And I can manage it because I have no illusions about my future with Septon. I do not need to be courted or to have a big ceremony to proclaim what I am to have with him. I have his ring and his word, and that will be enough.' And, though they had not spoken of it, she was sure she could convince Septon to honour her mother's debts. He might behave as horribly as he wished, so long as she did not have to see her mother living in a hovel and relying on the church for charity. Grim fears of this future had been keeping her up at night since Father's death, and with Septon's help, she would finally be free of them.

Perhaps that was the real source of the strange feeling that remained inside her, now that he was gone. She felt light-headed and tingly, as if an invisible breath was stirring the tiny hairs on her body, perhaps as a prelude to a kiss.

Septon's breath.

Septon's kiss.

She gave a little shudder to clear her mind of the thought and smiled at her mother encouragingly. 'You must learn to be grateful, you know. The Duke might be a bit of a rogue, but he is to be our salvation.

'Septon a saviour. That is ripe.' Her mother snorted. 'Since it seems there is no dissuading you, we will go ahead with this farce and get you properly married before he changes his mind. Until then, there will be absolutely no unchaperoned contact between you, lest he try to play you false and seek intimacy before it is his legal right.'

'Mother,' she warned, 'I seriously doubt that will be a problem.' All the same, her heart beat quicker at the thought that he might try to do something improper.

'I do not trust him and I never shall,' her mother said, eyes narrowing. 'But he is gone for now, and it gives us an excuse to go to Bond Street and celebrate your supposed good fortune.'

'Bond Street?' she replied, surprised. 'What do we need there?'

'You will want a new gown for the wedding,' her mother said. 'And a trousseau of some kind. You can't go to him in rags.'

Portia felt her nerves tighten again, at the thought of another of her mother's shopping sprees. She had spent the last eighteen months, trying to persuade the woman that they had no money to spend on frivolous purchases. She certainly did not want to incur any new debts before she had access to her husband's fortune and a way to pay for the purchases. 'The clothing I have already will serve well enough.'

'You do not want a new gown for the most important day of your life?' her mother said indignantly.

'Everything in my wardrobe was bought at the beginning of the Season, and some of the gowns have not yet been worn,' she said with a firm smile. 'And it is not as if the Duke will back down over the cut of my pelisse.' She raised her hand, displaying the betrothal ring with a flourish. 'He cannot exactly jilt me after giving me this.'

'No new gowns, then,' her mother said with a sigh. 'But you will need nightclothes. And underthings. Petticoats, shifts, stays…' She was counting off a list on her fingers that seemed far beyond what any reasonable person would need.

'Those will not be necessary either,' Portia said hurriedly. 'It is not as if such things are worn where anyone can see them, and what I have is all in good condition.'

'Your husband will see them,' her mother said stubbornly. 'And a man of his jaded tastes will have certain expectations.' She gave another disgusted sniff and added, 'We will send him the bills.'

'Certainly not,' Portia blurted, taking a deep breath before continuing. 'If he wants something of that nature, he can tell me himself, after we are married. He can pay the bills as well,' she added. 'But I refuse to incur expenses without consulting him.'

Her mother gave an exasperated huff. 'I am only trying to make sure that you use this union to your best advantage. If you mean to marry a cad and a bounder, you must learn to look out for yourself, Portia.'

'I am looking out for me,' she insisted, trying to ignore the nervous feeling that seemed to grow each time she spoke with her future husband. 'Really, I don't need much.'

'You do not understand at all what you have done,' her mother said for what seemed like the thousandth time. 'It is no longer about what you need, Portia. It is about what you deserve. As a duchess, you should have the best that Septon can afford to give you. You must take all you can get from him, for he will certainly take from you.'

She meant her maidenhead, Portia supposed, and remembered what Rose had said about talking to her mother. 'And what is it, precisely, that he will take from me?' Portia said, relieved to change the subject. 'You say he has jaded tastes, but what in? Not ladies' underthings, surely.'

The mercenary glint in her mother's eyes faded, and her cheeks flushed in embarrassment. 'When you are married, you will understand.'

'But I will have a far easier time of it if you explain now,' Portia replied coaxingly.

Her mother blinked. Opened her mouth to begin. Closed it again. Paused. And finally, when Portia was convinced that she would never speak, began slowly.

'There is a certain process that is done in the marital bed that results in children. Septon will have done this many times, with many more women than is proper and might have unusual opinions on the subject.'

'Then he must have many children,' Portia said, confused. 'But I have not read of any.'

'There are ways to prevent procreation,' her mother added vaguely. 'These other women are skilled in avoiding it. You do not need to know of those, since you want to have as many children as God and Septon will allow.'

Portia laughed. 'Since when does God allow Septon to help make decisions?'

'Sometimes the man withdraws,' her mother said, flushing even brighter.

'Withdraws what?' Portia said, even more confused than before.

Her mother swallowed nervously. 'There are probably books on the subject that will explain it better than I can.'

'I shall ask at Hatchards,' Portia said, relieved.

'No!' Her mother took a breath. 'I will find something for you. Do not go looking for answers on your own. It is probably better for you to be ignorant, since that is what Septon will be expecting. It will be proof of your innocence. That is what he wants, after all. An innocent wife.'

'Oh,' Portia said. Apparently, innocence and ignorance were in some way linked. She was certainly innocent of any useful facts on what was about to happen to her.

'I am glad we had this talk,' her mother said with a relieved sigh and rose. 'In any case, the wedding night should be the least of your worries. Septon has enough experience for both of you. Now let us go upstairs and choose your wedding dress. The blue muslin might be charming. Or perhaps the green.'

Portia followed her out of the room, unsure whether to hope or fear that her mother was correct.

Chapter Four

The wedding day arrived a week later, the licence having been procured without issue and the breakfast planned through a series of notes exchanged between Portia and the Duke's housekeeper, Mrs Gates. The woman had good handwriting and a no-nonsense manner that Portia decided was an encouraging sign for her future as mistress of Septon House. The master might be rackety in his manners, but his staff seemed competent, and she would likely see them more than she did her husband.

For the ceremony, she kept her word to her mother and chose the best of her current day gowns, a soft green muslin with embroidered flowers on the bodice. She did not bother with a veil but had Rose take extra care with her hair, curling it tightly and pinning it up behind a series of small braids. While she was getting married, the girl would see to the packing of her wardrobe for she would be following Portia to the new household to serve as her lady's maid.

'My mum is so proud,' she said, her eyes shining. 'Me, the personal servant to a duchess. She never dreamed…'

Portia smiled and nodded and wished her own mother was as pleased with this wedding as Rose's had been. When she went downstairs to call for the carriage, she was surprised to find a bouquet awaiting her in the front hall. It was a simple arrangement of white roses with a note attached that said, 'Regards, Septon.'

She ran her finger along the edge of the pasteboard, admiring the fine hand of the man who had sent it. His writing was strong and masculine with no blots or pauses in the lines. Two words were hardly a love note, but she appreciated them all the same. Since he had been adamant that they marry without fuss, she had not expected him to do anything.

She turned to her mother, holding the flowers up to show her after inhaling deeply of their perfume.

Her mother sniffed but made no effort to smell the flowers. 'It was the least he could do. After all, he has proved unwilling to pay for a proper ceremony in a church.'

'I do not think it was expense that concerned him,' Portia said. 'I think he values his privacy.'

'You think.' Her mother sniffed again. 'But you really have no idea, do you? You have only talked to him twice. For all we know, he may be avoiding the banns because he fears some common-law wife will appear to put a stop to the proceedings.'

'Mother,' she said, taking her firmest tone. 'He is to be family now and has done nothing to offend, as of yet.'

'Other than the duel that ruined you,' her mother reminded her.

'He has been more than willing to make up for that,' she said, trying not to think of the turmoil that had landed her here or the fact that when she'd gone to him with her remedy for it, he had never actually apologised. 'I wish to start this marriage on the right foot, and I cannot do so if you mean to accuse my new husband of crimes before he commits them. Please, moderate your behaviour so that we might get through the day without incident.'

Her mother huffed again and did not apologise either. But she made no further comment, only straightened the flowers on Portia's bonnet and announced that she looked quite lovely. Then they went out and got into the carriage the Duke had sent for the short ride to his townhouse.

They were let in by the butler, who gave Portia a long slow look and a nod of what seemed to be approval before bowing to her and leading her to the main salon, where the Duke and a vicar were waiting.

'Miss Braddock,' Septon said with a cool smile and a bow.

'Your Grace,' she said with a curtsey and a slight lift of the bouquet. 'I received your gift. It is quite lovely.'

He gave a dismissive wave of his hand. 'Something needed to be done to mark the occasion.' He glanced to her mother. 'Mrs Braddock. So good to see you again.'

Her mother said nothing in response, staring at him with a dour expression, then glancing around at the empty room as if to note the lack of guests.

'We are so happy to be here,' Portia said, stepping between them to answer for her. 'And this is such a lovely room. It is a charming place for a wedding.'

Her soon-to-be husband gave her a sceptical look. 'I am glad you both appreciate it.'

The vicar moved to join them, turning to her still-silent mother. 'We can start the ceremony as soon as the witnesses have arrived. Will you be fulfilling that duty for your daughter?'

Her mother looked around her again and said, 'If I must.'

The vicar turned to the Duke and said, 'Two witnesses are required.'

Portia looked at him as well, wondering why there

was no one to stand up for him. It was one thing to want a private ceremony and another to invite no one at all. She, at least, had her mother. But he was utterly alone.

For a moment an expression crossed Septon's face that might have been embarrassment. Then he walked to the bell-pull in the corner and rang twice.

A moment later, a woman that Portia suspected was the housekeeper appeared. 'Mrs Gates,' Septon said. 'Your presence is required. Someone must sign the licence.'

'Your Grace,' she said with a curtsey before offering Portia a curious look.

'This is to be your new mistress,' Septon added, with another awkward wave of his hand.

'Very good, Your Grace,' the woman said, her expression unwaveringly polite despite the unusual request.

Septon's face relaxed and he clapped his palms together as if to change the subject. 'Now that the witnesses are settled, let us begin.'

The vicar offered them both a dubious look as if he expected one or the other of them to call a halt and declare that this was nothing more than a joke. When met with silence, he opened his prayer book and began to read.

Portia had given little heed to the ceremony during the few weddings she'd been to in the past. When these words had not pertained to her, they'd seemed to be nothing more than a drawn-out ritual that stood between her and a hearty breakfast. But today, in this nearly empty room, she was painfully aware of each syllable, each word, each sentence.

In front of her, the vicar was droning on about the reasons for marriage and the fact that God was watching them at this very moment, judging their motives for being joined until death in his name. Portia swallowed nervously as he paused at the end of a phrase to peer over his book at her, as if waiting to see if her nerves would break and make her admit that she did not want to do this at all.

She held her breath and held her ground as the topic changed to procreation, another difficult subject that she did not fully understand. She had promised Septon an heir when she'd first come to him, so at least she meant well. But there was also something about the avoidance of fornication. Did that apply to both of them, she wondered? If she meant to ignore Septon's infidelities, was she breaking some sort of vow, or was it superseded by the requirement to be an obedient wife?

As for the exhortation to mutual society, comfort and help? If they barely saw each other, how would that work? None of this service pertained to her real reasons for marriage, which were largely financial. And God well knew it, if he knew the secrets of all hearts. Perhaps, when it came time to say her vows, she would be struck dead on the spot for being unworthy of the sacrament.

Her soon-to-be husband seemed to have no such doubts. As they reached the 'wilt thous' she glanced to him and he seemed…

Bored. She stared at him in amazement. He answered in the affirmative, as he had promised to, but it appeared he was completely unmoved by the ceremony. This was a life-changing event, even for a duke. Was he even listening to what the vicar was saying?

'Miss Braddock?'

She turned back to the man in front of her, who was looking expectantly at her, and realised that she had missed the question he had just addressed to her.

'I will?' she said, unable to keep the doubt from her voice.

The vicar nodded approvingly and turned to Septon, coaching him through the words he was expected to repeat. He spoke the vows in an emotionless voice, then reached in his pocket for a broad gold band, slipping it on her finger with barely a glance in her direction.

She stared at it for a moment, wondering if it was a family heirloom as the betrothal ring had been. It was heavy on her hand, probably expensive. Just another reminder of the weight of obligation she had accepted in exchange for gold.

The vicar had paused again. The room was silent, as if waiting for something, or someone.

Probably her.

Pay attention.

She looked up at the priest with a hopeful smile and he repeated the line for her.

She pushed through her part of the vows, reciting flawlessly and slumping in exhaustion when she was through. The promises had been made and she had survived. They were almost done.

And yet, the vicar did not stop. There were psalms and prayers that went on and on. The room, which had seemed chill when she'd entered it, was close and uncomfortable. And then, just when she thought it could not be much longer, the vicar took a deep breath and began a homily.

'That will be sufficient,' the Duke cut in.

The vicar looked up in confusion.

'We are well aware of our responsibilities as husband and wife and have made our promises,' he said in a firm voice. 'Please conclude the ceremony.'

When he'd come to her with his conditions and said that he wanted no moralising, she had thought him rude. But now that the moment was upon them, she felt nothing but relief. If she heard one more word about what she should or shouldn't be doing, she doubted that she could hold back a scream.

In front of her, the vicar gave the Duke a frightened look and, without another word, flipped ahead to the closing prayer, then pronounced them man and wife.

Without waiting for further instruction, the Duke turned to her and kissed her on the lips.

The kiss was done before she had a chance to form an opinion about it. In retrospect, it seemed as passionless and efficient as a handshake. But what had she expected from the stranger she'd married?

Something more, she realised. He was supposed to be an infamous rake, a despoiler of innocents. Now that she was legally in his clutches, she did not feel the least bit despoiled. She felt untouched by emotion of any kind. It was probably just as well. She had not expected him to seduce her in the drawing room with the vicar standing right next to them. But lingering a moment over their first kiss might have given the impression that this was a love match and not the passionless arrangement that it was likely to be.

'Very good,' her husband said, with a smile as cold and businesslike as the kiss had been. 'Let us go into breakfast.' He looked to the housekeeper and said, 'You are dismissed, Mrs Gates.'

'Yes, Your Grace,' she said, standing beside the sitting room door as they walked through it and down the hall.

He turned back to Portia and offered his arm to escort her.

She looked at it for a moment, her mind a blank. Then she remembered that, though this was now her home, she did not even know the way to the dining room. So she took it and allowed herself to be led.

In the dining room, Julian sat mute as the meal was served, staring down the table at the flowers that the housekeeper had chosen to decorate the cloth, the crystal glasses of champagne sparkling in the morning sun, and the vicar and his mother-in-law seated on either side of the table.

Anywhere but at his bride.

He was not used to feeling so unsettled in the presence of a woman. If he'd wanted to get one into his bed before today, he'd always had the right word, the right smile and charm. So much charm. But he'd never thought that he would use those skills on Portia Braddock, or that the matter of her consent would be settled before he'd even had to make a veiled suggestion that they let the night take them where it would.

He would be bedding her tonight. She knew it. He knew it. Everyone in the house knew. Even the vicar.

God help him, if he looked at her, he was afraid he was going to blush, and he had never done that in his life.

It was either that or cast the others out of the room and have her on the breakfast table like the rogue he was. He could not trust his mind in the presence of Portia Braddock. Portia Parish, rather. His wife.

He took a deep drink of his wine and told himself firmly that it was too early to be thinking of activities that should take place after dark in the marital bed. But it seemed that the whole of the wedding ceremony had been designed to remind him of coupling. If they had been marrying for love, things would be different. They would both be looking forward to their first night together.

Instead, his brain was clouded by lust, and she had sworn that she felt nothing for him at all. She probably viewed what was to come as a duty, unseemly perhaps, but a task she had promised to complete so she might get what she wanted out of him.

He signalled to a servant to refill his champagne glass and wished for something stronger.

'It is a lovely breakfast.'

His wife was speaking to him, the words tickling along his spine like fingers. He could not very well ignore her, so he forced himself to glance in her direction and said, 'You have Mrs Gates to thank for that. She arranged it all.'

Did she feel disappointment that he was not in some way involved? If so, then how had she felt when he'd forgotten to invite a witness to their wedding? She was probably just as embarrassed as he was that he had no friends that he might want to see in daylight, with a preacher present.

Well, one, perhaps. Since George had died, Westbridge had taken his place as Julian's closest confidant. Until recently, they had been almost like brothers. But skewering him on his sword's point had likely put an end to that friendship. At the very least, it would have made a wedding invitation awkward.

At least he had remembered the ring. He glanced down at her hand, which was resting on the stem of her wine glass, fascinated by the fingers and their fine tapered nails. He could imagine the scrape of them against his skin, every part of him alert with desire.

She noticed the direction of his gaze and spoke. 'Was it your mother's ring?'

'No,' he said, trying not to shudder at the thought. He wanted no part of his parents in this union and wished to pretend, at least for a while, that all women were not alike. He had gone to Bond Street just yesterday and had sought something new that would not remind him of the past.

'Well, it is lovely, all the same,' she said with a wistful sigh.

Did she like it? He wondered what she had been expecting. Probably something larger, with a diamond that could be seen from across a crowded ballroom.

He had agonised over the decision, shocked at how alike all the rings were and imagining that one in the bunch might be in some way luckier than the others. In the end, he had chosen the first one he'd looked at, assuming that that was some sort of sign. It was a simple gold band engraved with a pattern of flowers that the jeweller had said were forget-me-nots.

Judging by her reaction, he had chosen wrong.

Down the table from her, her mother was eyeing him with suspicion. The woman made no effort to hide the fact that she loathed him, which made her much easier to deal with. He gave her a direct look and asked, 'Is the breakfast to your liking as well?'

'Very fine, thank you,' she replied in a clipped tone that said just the opposite of her words.

Her daughter sensed it as well and inserted herself into the conversation. 'I have never tasted such a delicious sauce on the salmon.' She let out a small, nervous laugh. 'I was about to ask after the recipe. But I suppose, if I am to live here now, that is not necessary.'

'Capers,' her mother said in the same blunt manner. 'I am sure you have had them before.'

'Perhaps. But they are particularly good today,' Portia insisted and gave him an apologetic smile. 'Has your housekeeper been with you long?'

'All the senior staff have been with the house since my father was alive,' he said. 'The butler, Banks, was here when I was born.'

'He must be very protective of you,' she said with a smile.

'I suppose,' he said, glancing towards the doorway where the servant was standing, wearing his usual expression of disapproval. If Julian was honest with himself, the butler's scorn was well-deserved. He had been a disappointment as both a man and a peer, and Banks's standards were exceptionally high.

'It was most kind of Mrs Gates to help us with the wedding,' Portia said, trying to fill the silence between them.

'It is her job to do as I say,' he said, embarrassed to be reminded of his earlier mistake.

'It was kind of her, all the same,' she said, still smiling. 'And it's good to know that you have such a loyal and competent staff.

'They are your staff now, as well,' her mother reminded her. She glared in Julian's direction. 'Keep a firm hand on them, for if they are anything like their master, they are not to be trusted with the silver.'

Across the table from her, the vicar gasped but said nothing.

As Julian prepared a response, his new wife broke the silence. 'Do not talk nonsense, Mother.' Out of the corner of his eye, he saw her looking nervously in his direction by way of apology.

It was probably too much to expect that she leap to his defence. He had done nothing to earn her respect, nor did he plan to do anything in the future. He took a sip of wine, then looked to her mother with a smile. 'I do not fear for my silver, madam. When one is able to pay their staff, they do not have problems with disloyalty.'

His mother-in-law spluttered, and beside him, Portia flushed in embarrassment. But at least they were silent and he was able to finish his salmon in peace.

The meal dragged on for some time and ended with a wedding cake rich with dried fruit and nuts and decorated with marzipan flowers. As she had with all the other courses, his new wife remarked on the quality of the baking, and his new mother-in-law expressed her apathy.

He ate his piece quickly, eager to put an end to the ordeal and rid his house of guests. But when they had finished the dessert and proceeded to the front hall to say their goodbyes, Mrs Braddock lingered on the doorstep after the vicar had gone, as if she did not want to leave.

Without warning, she let out a wail and threw herself into her daughter's arms. She lifted her head and gave him an accusing glare, her eyes dry and her lips twisted in a sneer. 'I don't want to leave you in this horrible place,' she moaned into Portia's shoulder. 'It will all end in tears.'

'Now, Mother,' she said, giving Julian a desperate look. 'Do not be silly. I was bound to marry, eventually. Sooner, rather than later.'

'But not to him,' she said, with another false sob. 'He is no better than your father, and we all know how that ended.'

His wife was looking at him now, silently pleading with him to say something reassuring. But what if he agreed with her mother? This was a disaster waiting to happen and he was destined to make his wife as disappointed and miserable as everyone else who had counted on him to be better than he was.

He gave a helpless shrug, then forced out the words. 'Do not worry, Mrs Braddock, your daughter will want for nothing.' That was vague, but true, he supposed. 'You have my word.'

'The word of a gentleman?' her mother said, wiping away her non-existent tears with the handkerchief that her daughter was forcing on her. 'Well then. I have nothing to worry about.' It was said with the same scorn as all her other comments.

If he'd had any pride left to wound, the words might

have stung. But fighting with her would only prolong the visit, so he allowed it to pass without comment and took a step closer to the open door.

After a final, ominous look at her daughter and Portia's continued assurances that all would be well, they bid adieu and Mrs Braddock left them alone in the hall.

It was just the two of them, at last. The moment he had been waiting for since the ceremony. But the passionate fire that had burned in him earlier in the day had been doused by her mother's pointed reminders that he was unworthy of Portia's affections. As the footman closed the door, an awkward silence fell between them.

'I am sorry that you had to witness that,' his wife said in a small voice. 'My mother does not always think before she speaks.'

Julian was tempted to announce that this was a colossal understatement. But if he was honest, with the reputation he had built for himself, he was not every mother's prayer for a son-in-law. After considering in silence for a moment, he said, 'We will speak no more about it. But I will tolerate no further scenes in the future. To prevent them, I would prefer that, if you wish your mother to visit you here, you wait until I am out of the house.' With luck, he would never have to see the woman again.

Portia's eyes widened slightly, and her lips parted as if she wished to argue. Then she closed them again and nodded.

'Thank you,' he said, glad that the matter was settled.

She was still staring at him, as if she expected him to say something more. When he did not, she smiled and looked around her, then said, 'The ceremony is over and the guests are gone. But I have no idea what is to happen next. Do you?'

Bed.

There it was again, the thought that had plagued him since the first day he'd met her. But to speak it aloud the first minute they were alone would make him seem as bad as her mother thought he was. He could not fall on her like some ravening beast that had no respect for her innocence. He should at least wait until after dinner. Then he would take his time with her and see that the experience was a pleasant one.

But that was half a day away. What were they to do until then? She, at least, could be kept busy with household duties. 'You have much to learn if you are to be mistress here,' he said. 'I will summon Mrs Gates, who will give you a tour of the house and show you to your rooms.'

'And you?' she said, with that same earnest smile.

He could not think of a thing. He always found

something to do at night, but his days were empty. He'd never had anyone here to see just how feckless he really was. 'I am going out,' he said. 'I will return for supper.' God knew where he would go, for he had no business to complete and Parliament was not in session today. But he did not think he could maintain control, knowing that she was in the house and there was nothing standing between them and intimacy but his fragile willpower.

'Very well,' she said, her smile fading just a little as he rang for the housekeeper and told a footman to bring his hat and gloves. Then he was out of the house and could pretend, if only for an afternoon, that his life had not changed into something he could no longer understand.

Chapter Five

Portia watched as the door closed after her retreating husband, and turned to the housekeeper, only half listening to her well wishes.

Would Septon always be so quiet, she wondered? He had been largely silent through the ceremony and breakfast, his expression detached, his smiles never reaching his eyes. When she had managed to get him to answer a question, she was surprised to find that her new ring had not belonged to his mother. She'd imagined that, as duchess, she would wear some piece of entailed jewellery, like the betrothal ring had been. Apparently, that was not to be.

Perhaps there was a limit to her place in this family. She was not really his first choice of bride, after all. She wondered if there was someone he'd have rather given his mother's ring to, someone he had an actual fondness for.

The fact that he'd left her immediately after the

wedding seemed to support this. After the scenes her mother had made at breakfast and in the hall, he could not get away fast enough. But before he'd left, he'd told her that her mother was not welcome in his home whenever he was present.

What had her mother been thinking? If she wished him to pay the Braddock family bills, they depended on the Duke's goodwill. Mother had squandered that before the cake was even cut. How was Portia to convince him to care for a woman who so obviously held him in such contempt?

And just where had he gone in such a hurry? A gambling hell? A brothel? Were such places even open in daylight? He could not be wicked all hours of the day, could he? She'd known she was marrying a stranger. But she had assumed that, once they were alone together, he would at least make some effort to become better acquainted with her.

Apparently not.

'Would you like me to assemble the staff?' Mrs Gates had completed her introduction, and Portia had not heard a word of it. Worse yet, she'd done nothing to hide her distraction. She must remember that she had promised the Duke she would not meddle in his affairs. If she was wondering at his absence on the very first day, she was already failing.

She focused her attention on the housekeeper. 'That

would be most helpful.' Then she admitted, 'You will likely have to tell me their names several times over. It is all rather overwhelming, today.'

'It is your wedding day,' the woman said with a sympathetic smile. 'I expect you have much on your mind.' She went to the bell-pull and signalled the staff to come up from below stairs.

As the servants assembled before her, she tried not to be intimidated. Her mother had managed quite well with a housekeeper, a cook and a pair of maids, one of whom Portia had brought with her to this house. But Septon had footmen, parlour maids, a valet, a butler, a housekeeper and a cook and her accompanying scullery maids. Now they were all staring at her as if trying to decide whether she was worthy of their obedience.

She turned to the butler, who stood at the head of the row and gave him what she hoped was an authoritative smile. 'It must be quite a change, having a mistress of the house, Banks. His Grace was a perennial bachelor, after all.'

'I would not presume to have an opinion, Your Grace,' he said automatically. The words were proper enough, but there was something about the look on his face, a certain arch of the eyebrow and set of the lips, which made her suspect he was lying. He was full to the brim with opinions. He simply had no intention of sharing them with a woman who had arrived in the house only hours ago.

She nodded in response and said, 'You needn't worry about my plans for the future. I do not approve of change for change's sake, nor do I wish to upend a household as well-run as this one seems to be.'

His mouth twitched at the corner, but he said, 'Very good, Your Grace,' and stared straight ahead.

What was she to make of this? His words were straightforward and ordinary, and yet, somehow wrong. She could not help but feel that there was a change he had very much hoped to see her make. But she had no idea what it might be, and he had no intention of telling her directly.

She stared at him for a moment longer, but it was like trying to read the unreadable. She liked puzzles. She simply had not expected to find one hidden amongst the staff on her very first day here. She turned away from him and smiled down the row of servants. 'Thank you all for your hard work. I will not keep you from it any longer.' She paused for a moment, wondering if she dared make a decision without consulting her new husband, then pushed ahead and announced, 'In celebration of the occasion, you will all receive an extra week's pay.'

A surprised gasp went up from the assembly. Then

it was just as quickly stifled. 'Thank you, Your Grace,' said Mrs Gates.

'You are all most welcome,' she said, then added, 'I think I would like to go to my room now and see to the unpacking. If you would be so kind as to show me the way?'

'Of course, Your Grace,' she said, dispersing the servants with a gesture of her hand and turning towards the stairs.

Portia followed her, relieved. Perhaps bribery was not the best way to earn the loyalty of a household, but it was both quick and effective and would ease the sting of the mistakes she was sure to make when getting used to the running of the house. She hoped nothing more would be expected of her this day for she doubted she had the strength for it.

Then she remembered her husband and the fact that there was a duty she had yet to perform with him that was a complete mystery to her. But if it was done while in bed, it couldn't be too terribly strenuous, could it? She tried and failed to control the nervous shiver that went through her as they crossed the threshold to her room.

'You are tired,' Mrs Gates said with a sympathetic smile. 'I will send up some tea and cakes. You must rest until dinner. It will be a long night, after all.'

'I suppose it will,' Portia said, trying not to blush.

The housekeeper left her, and she slipped out of her shoes and climbed into bed to wait for her tea.

Julian returned to the house at half past seven, which allowed just enough time to dress for dinner. After escaping the house after the wedding, he'd spent the day in idleness, much as he spent most of his days. He'd begun with a long walk, having little choice in the matter, since he'd sent the carriage away to take the abhorrent Mrs Braddock to her home. Judging by her comments earlier in the day, he suspected it would have given her great pleasure to know that she had inconvenienced him.

The exercise had been good for him, calming his nerves and cooling his blood until he felt something akin to normal. He might almost have been able to forget the dramatic turn his life had taken, but for the congratulations he'd received when he settled down at White's with a brandy and a copy of *The Times*.

Men who had been calling him a danger to society and demanding his arrest just a few days ago, were now smiling and nodding knowingly, as if the duel made perfect sense to them. A man could not be blamed for acting rashly when the love of his life was defamed. Westbridge had got what he deserved for poking a sleeping tiger and speaking out of turn about the new Duchess of Septon.

He had a good mind to tell them that this marriage

had been her idea, and that he'd had no such thing on his mind when he'd issued the challenge. But for a change, he remembered the saying about discretion and valour and kept his mouth shut, accepting the well wishes with a grim smile and changing the subject when he could.

When he returned to the townhouse, he was exhausted and wishing that he had allowed time for a nap before dinner. Instead, he splashed his face with water from the wash basin and called for his valet, who had already laid out his dinner clothes.

He would be tired, after he visited his wife's bedchamber tonight. For a change, he might be able to sleep until morning. If marriage banished his insomnia, even for a night or two, it might not be as bad as he expected.

When he went down to the dining room half an hour later, it was to find his wife already seated at the table in a copper-coloured gown, cut low to reveal the gentle curves of her breasts. She looked up at him with an undisguised eagerness that he had not expected. She had seemed ambivalent to him when she'd first come to him, but today, she was different.

This new warmth was probably false, put on to make up for her mother's antipathy. If so, it was working just as she'd hoped. His fatigue evaporated; his body aware of hers as it always was when he was near to her.

'Good evening, Your Grace,' she said with a smile. And for a moment, he was at a loss for words. She was still staring at him, waiting for a response.

His mouth went dry, the glib reply he'd meant to make flying right out of his head. 'Good evening,' he managed at last, taking his seat at the head of the table. 'And, given the circumstances, you should probably call me Julian.'

'Thank you, Julian,' she said, obediently.

The sound of his name played on his nerves like a caress. He took a sip of wine and signalled for the first course to be served.

'How was your day?' she enquired, obviously uncomfortable with the silence.

Empty without you.

He was not about to admit that he had spent the hours waiting for the moment he could return to her. Such an admission would give her an advantage over him that he did not want to cede on the very first day of their marriage. 'Uneventful,' he said, offering no further information. 'And yours?' Their eyes met and he held her gaze, feeling his confidence return as she blinked back at him, wide-eyed and flustered.

Her eyes were her best feature, he decided. He had thought of them as gold, but they were rimmed in green, which became more noticeable when her pupils were large, as they were tonight. He was tempted to say something shocking, just to watch them change.

But a shock was hardly necessary for she had been stunned to silence with a single glance. 'Your day,' he said softly. 'How was it?'

She blinked again before saying, 'Fine. Very good. Mrs Gates showed me the house and introduced me to the servants.' Her hands fluttered for a moment before settling on the silverware, gripping the handles tightly as if they could anchor her in her place.

'And what did you make of them?' he replied, taking a slow sip of his wine and watching the colour rise in her cheeks. Were her breasts flushed as well, he wondered? He would see soon enough.

She hazarded another glance in his direction, peering at him through her lashes before looking down at her plate again. 'They are very well-trained. You have a lovely home. Very well-kept.' She took a hurried bite of food, chewing as if she was glad of an excuse not to talk.

'It is your home now, as well,' he said. Then he added, 'But?'

She looked up, startled.

'You have changes you want to make, I assume,' he said, giving her a searching look. 'The house has not been redecorated in years. New furniture. New curtains. Hangings for the beds…' Now that she was a duchess, it was only a matter of time before she began altering his life and home to suit her desires. He had watched his mother run through hundreds of pounds in a single day, trying to stay ahead of the latest fashions.

But his new wife was blinking at him, baffled. 'It looks fine to me. Far grander than I am used to. But if there is something that you want me to change…'

He stared at her, searching for sarcasm or subterfuge. A more experienced woman would know how to barter her favours for the things she wanted. But she was still innocent and not likely to refuse him tonight, of all nights.

'The decoration of this house is neither here nor there for me,' he said. 'After you have spoken with some of the other women of your set, you will likely change your mind.' That was what women did, after all. They were as changeable as the wind.

She took a sip of her wine and gave him another guarded look, biting her lip as if deciding whether she should speak. Did she know it formed her mouth into a kissable pout?

Before he could lean forward and show her, she said, 'I did do something that I am not sure you will approve of.'

'Really.' He set his fork down and waited.

'I promised the staff an extra week's pay so that they could celebrate the wedding,' she said.

Of all things, he had not expected that her first act as his wife would be to think of the needs of others. 'I should have done that myself,' he admitted, embarrassed that he had not. 'They have been working twice as hard to prepare for your arrival. It is only fair that we compensate them for it.'

She relaxed in her seat, smiling. 'I am glad you think so.' She took another bite of the ragout of lamb they'd been served and he watched in fascination as she licked the gravy from her lips. 'And one thing I am sure I will not change is your cook. The meals I have had here are excellent.'

'I had not noticed,' he said, still thinking about her mouth.

'Perhaps it is because you have known nothing else,' she said. 'Since Father died, we've had to make do with mutton.' She took another bite, closed her eyes and gave a little moan of pleasure as she chewed.

His loins tightened at the sound, and he took another sip of wine. If the gods were kind, she would be as responsive in the bedroom as she was at the table. When she swallowed and opened her eyes, he took a morsel of meat onto his fork and reached across to offer it to her.

She looked confused for a moment, then accepted

it, the fork sliding into her mouth and reappearing empty a moment later.

Her obedient response raised a slew of possibilities, none of which he could carry out in the dining room with footmen present and Banks smirking just outside the door. For now, he said, 'Be sure to tell Cook if there is anything particular that you desire.'

'I will do that,' she said. 'But I need to know your favourites as well. What do you wish to see on the menu?'

'I am not usually at home for dinner,' he said, clearing the last of his plate as the next course was brought.

'Oh.' Her face fell and she busied herself with finishing her lamb.

'When I am home, I leave it up to Mrs Gates to set the menu,' he added. 'She will tell you what is regularly served.'

'She is very helpful,' she said, pushing her plate away as dessert was served, a savoy cake soaked with honey and decorated with figs. She stared at it, with an amazed smile. 'How lovely.'

He offered her another forkful and stared at the honey glistening on her lips as she ate. 'It is a wedding gift from Cook, I think. Honey and figs are known for their ability to enflame the passions.'

She stopped chewing and looked down at her plate in alarm.

'Eat up,' he said. 'It is almost time for bed.'

Chapter Six

Her fork clattered onto her dessert plate, making a deafening noise in the silence of the dining room. 'So soon?' she said, embarrassed at the squeaky, nervous pitch of her voice.

'Did you have something else you wished to do?' he asked, giving her another searching look. He had been staring at her for the whole meal, and it was almost as disconcerting as his neglect had been at breakfast.

'It has been a very tiring day,' she said, and felt stupid for it. She was sure he was not talking about going to sleep, and it must make her sound like a ninny to imply such. His fork appeared in front of her again, and she took the cake from it, wondering if he took some pleasure in feeding her or was simply trying to hurry the meal to a conclusion.

For a moment, she considered begging for a reprieve. Just a night or two to get used to her new home before the real business of marriage began. She did not know him. They had never even been alone together. Even during this first meal, there were footmen going in and out, setting plates and filling glasses.

If she begged for more time, those same servants would overhear. Then there would be gossip below stairs that the new mistress had refused her husband. Her timidity would shame him and make things even more difficult when he did come to her.

She watched as he ate a fig, licking away the juice on his bottom lip. It was strangely disconcerting, and she closed her eyes so she would not have to see. 'I have never done this before,' she blurted. 'I do not even know...' She took another bite of cake wishing that she had not spoken at all.

'I am aware of that,' he said, his fork scraping on an empty plate. 'But I have.'

She chewed and swallowed, chewed and swallowed, trying not to think of what her mother had said about rakes and their sinful behaviour. When she looked down, there was nothing left on her plate but a drizzle of honey. She debated asking for a second slice, then dipped her fingertip in the remaining syrup and licked it clean.

Beside her, she heard a gasp of surprise.

He was probably thinking she had atrocious manners. She wiped her hand clean and stood. Then she looked at him, forcing a smile. 'I will go to my room and prepare for bed.' Before she could embarrass herself further, she hurried out of the room and up the stairs, relieved to find her maid already waiting for her.

Rose was laying out one of the new nightgowns that her mother had insisted she buy, shaking out the wrinkles and holding it up to the light to reveal the sheerness of the fabric. 'This one is the finest, Your Grace,' she said, with an impish grin. 'Such a pretty thing. And it has little bows that will come undone with no trouble at all.'

'Whatever you think is best,' Portia said, going to sit at the dressing table without another look. She added, 'It is not really necessary to make a grand show of things. I doubt it matters to Septon what I look like. He married me, and that is proof enough that he is willing to...' She gave a little shrug.

Rose came to stand behind her and began to undo the pins in her hair. 'Perhaps that is so. But some men like it when you make a bit of effort to show you are willing.'

'I promised I was,' Portia said firmly. 'That should be enough.'

'And you had the talk with your mother that we discussed?' the maid asked, pausing with hairbrush in mid stroke to stare into her reflected eyes.

In answer, Portia could do nothing but blush.

Rose nodded in approval. 'That is good. I am sure it will not be as bad as your mother made it sound. It only hurts the first time, after all.'

'It hurts?' Portia said, turning back to look at her directly.

Rose looked back at her alarmed. 'Only the first time. And not always. It depends.'

'Depends on what?' Portia demanded.

'On the position, and the man involved. And his size.'

'Size?' Now she sounded shrill, but she could not help it. Septon was over six feet and quite the tallest man she'd ever met. It would have been better if her mother had said something about this before she'd gone to him. But instead, she had yammered on about his reputation and said nothing about what physical difficulty his height might cause.

Before she could ask for further explanation, there was a knock on the door that connected to the Duke's room. He opened it without waiting for an answer and came into her room, leaning against the doorframe and staring in her direction.

She stared back at him, terrified. She had barely left the dining room, where he had still been finishing his wine. But now, he was wearing a blue silk dressing gown, tied tightly at the waist and she could see by the vee of bare skin at his throat, and the naked feet and ankles protruding at the hem that there was no nightshirt beneath it. How had he changed so quickly? And why?

Without thinking, she raised one hand to clutch the neckline of her gown, as if it was necessary to shield her still clothed body from his gaze.

He smiled back at her, staring at the hand until she dropped it into her lap again. Then he turned to Rose and gave her a different, matter-of-fact look. 'You are dismissed.'

The girl curtsied and giggled, giving Portia a parting smile before disappearing out of the door and shutting it behind her.

The Duke shut the door behind him as well, leaving the two of them truly alone for the first time.

'I was not finished preparing for bed,' Portia said, turning back to the mirror, reaching for her brush, and giving her hair a few ineffectual strokes.

'I am quite capable of taking care of that for you,' he said, his eyes growing dark and bottomless. 'In fact, I would prefer to do so.' He approached her from behind, took the brush from her hands and set it aside. He wound the length of her hair around his hand before letting the locks fall through his fingers to hang down her back, then swept it over her shoulder and began undoing the fastenings of her bodice.

'That is not necessary,' she said hurriedly, clutching at her gown again as it began to slip from her shoulders.

'You wish me to take you as you are?' he said, giving her a smile that could only be described as rakish. 'That will not be as pleasant for either of us. I do not want to begin our married life on a false note.'

'It will not be pleasant for me in any case,' she said, thinking of what Rose had told her and swallowing nervously.

Was it her imagination or did he suddenly look worried as well? Then his smile returned. 'So you think. But I have a certain reputation to uphold, and I will see to it that the night will not be without pleasure.'

'It might be easier if you just do what it is that you came here to do and get it over with,' she said, her fingers tightening on the cloth of the bodice. 'I will not refuse you. And it is not as if we love each other. Do not feel that you must act any differently on my account.'

He laughed, surprised. 'I do not know what you have been told about tonight, but you should probably let me decide how best to proceed.' He reached down to undo the last buttons of her gown. 'The first thing you will learn is that we do not need to love each other to have a delightful evening.' He untied the knot of her stays and made short work of the lacing. 'Affection is helpful, of course. But not necessary for what I have in mind.'

He put a hand on each of her shoulders and pushed gown and stays down her arms. Then he clasped the hand that still held her clothing to her body and brought it to his lips before slipping her sleeve over her fingers and off. The clothing pooled in her lap, leaving her bare to the waist, except for her shift. When she looked in the mirror, she could see the outline of her breasts, pressing against the thin linen.

So could he. His gaze lowered to admire them as his hands stroked her bare arms. 'You will find that, when passions are aroused, love and hate and all the other emotions become secondary to the moment.'

She swallowed again, suddenly aware of how little she had understood, when she'd asked for this marriage. How foolish had she been to think that this wolf would bend tamely to her direction?

One of his hands had gone back to stroking her hair, and he raised a lock to his face, inhaling its fragrance before letting it fall in front of her. 'You do have the most marvellous hair, my dear. So soft. So smooth. And long enough to conceal your breasts. When we are alone together, it must always be loose, just like this.'

'If you wish,' she said, relieved that his first request was an easy one.

His hands came up to her shoulders again and his fingers dug into the tight muscles, working small circles in them until she began to relax. Almost against her will, she found herself leaning into the caress.

He sighed in approval. 'There, you see? We cannot just "get it over with," as you suggested. If you simply wanted to copulate, you should have chosen one of those bloodless boys that were courting you earlier in the Season. They'd have been finished with you before they even messed up your hair.

'Copulate?' she said trying to pull away. The word was as strange and unfamiliar as everything else about this evening.

He was definitely laughing now, releasing little puffs of air as he nuzzled the back of her neck. 'Copulate,' he repeated, letting her feel each syllable against her skin. 'Such a clinical way to describe it.' His hands skimmed her sides and reached around her to cover her breasts. 'Fornicate. Couple. Join.' He was stoking her nipples through her shift, teasing them with his nails and rolling them between his fingers. 'I will teach you other words to describe what we do together, ones that cannot be used in polite society.'

'I should not think I will be needing those,' she said nervously. Then she took a deep breath and tried to ignore what his hands were doing to her.

'You will,' he insisted. 'I mean to teach you everything you need to know so you might ask for pleasure from your lovers.'

'Lovers?' she said shocked.

He gave her nipples a hard tweak that made her gasp with pleasure. 'After you bear me a son or two, you can seek satisfaction where you like. But I hope you will know better than to go to someone too selfish to please you.'

How could he talk like this while touching her in this way? She wanted to be angry that he was thinking of the end even before there was a beginning. But the sensations rushing through her were like a tide carrying her helplessly out to sea. This was not love. They both knew that. But he'd said that did not matter.

'I will teach you everything you need to know,' he said again, pulling her to her feet and holding her against him for a moment. Then he undid her petticoat and pushed it and the gown to the floor, leaving her in nothing but shift and stockings, standing before the mirror.

He held her hips now, moulding them against him, and she felt something hard pressing into her bottom. He was staring into her eyes, reflected in the mirror. As he did so, the strangest feeling seemed to grow in the pit of her stomach. It was not quite fear. Anticipation, she decided, though she was still not sure for what.

He was smiling again, his gaze skimming down her body like a gentle touch. 'How innocent you look, my dear, in shift and stockings.' The pressure against her bottom increased as he rocked his hips into hers. 'I have never been so hard.'

Before she could think of a response, he swept a hand across the dressing table scattering pins and brushes to the floor. Then he grabbed her by the waist and set her on top of it, stepping around the little bench to sit between her legs. He hooked a hand behind one of her knees and brought her foot up and placed it on the bench beside him.

Cautiously, she raised the other leg to match it. As she did so, her shift rode up and she grabbed the hem, trying to tug it down again, barely sure of what she was trying to protect.

'No,' he said, wagging a finger at her, then eased her legs even further apart. 'I only wish to help with your stockings.' He dipped his head and took the end of a garter in his teeth, untying the bow. His hands smoothed the silk of the stocking down her calf to her foot, cradling the sensitive arch in his hand before sliding the sock away and letting it fall to the floor. Then he turned his head and began the process with her other stocking.

The little nips of his teeth against her thigh were maddening, making her squirm with pleasure.

'You are making this harder than it needs to be,' he said, laughing against her skin and gripping her leg firmly. He sucked the flesh of her thigh into his mouth, teasing her with his teeth and tongue.

She bit her lip to muffle a moan and leaned back on her hands, arching her back, giving in to the kiss, helpless to resist him.

When he was finished, he caught the garter in his teeth again and pulled it away. Stripping the stocking off and giving her the same, dark hungry look he had given her before. 'You like it when I kiss you there?'

She nodded hesitantly.

He smoothed his hands up her legs to the place where they joined. 'Perhaps you would enjoy it if I kissed you here.'

'You mustn't,' she said, sitting up and trying to pull the shift down again.

'*Mustn't* is not a word we use in the bedroom,' he said. 'I will if you wish me to, after I have kissed you everywhere else and you ask me nicely.'

'I would never,' she said.

At this, he simply laughed and bit her thigh, again.

She jumped at the sensation, then forced herself to be still, for she did not think she wanted him to stop.

His hands, which had retreated when she'd drawn away, moved higher, settling between her legs again. 'Do you ever touch yourself here?' he said, his finger drawing a line that dipped briefly into the opening of her body.

She gasped and shook her head.

His eyes widened. 'I knew you were innocent, but I had no idea… Let me show you.' His hands began to move on her, feather light strokes of the little bud between her legs. He bent forward hovering over her for a moment before his mouth settled on one of her breasts, sucking the nipple through the linen of her shift keeping time with the rhythm of his hands.

He paused the kiss, laying his head against her breast. 'Tell me how to please you. Tell me what you like.'

She closed her eyes, afraid to look at him, and focused on his touch. It made her feel strange, as if she was opening like a flower. It felt wonderful, but also dangerous, like a storm she couldn't control. Was it supposed to be this way? How was she to guide him if she didn't know where they were going?

He sensed her confusion and gathered up one of her hands, leading it back to her own body. 'Touch yourself, as I was touching you.'

She stared at him in the reflection, shocked. 'I…'

'No,' he said again, laying a finger against her lips to silence her. 'You were going to say "shouldn't" again, weren't you?'

She nodded.

He moved her hand so the fingertips brushed her tender flesh. 'Do as I ask.'

Hesitantly, she moved her fingers, searching for the place he had been touching.

'Play,' he commanded.

This was wicked, she was sure, and nothing like she'd expected. But he was holding her tightly, one hand still over her mouth, the other clutching her hip, dominating her easily as she fumbled to find her pleasure.

'Imagine my lips on you,' he said. 'Imagine me entering you. Imagine my cock filling you.'

Her breath quickened, as she stared into his eyes, so large and dark and unreadable. He was smiling as if he knew things that she did not, and his finger left her lips and drew a new line down her body, between her breasts and lower to the place where her fingers were hesitantly brushing the tight knot of nerves between her legs. Then his fingers slid past and inside, filling her as he had described.

The strange sensation she had been feeling changed to an urgent need and without thinking, she stroked herself in time to the movement of his hand. She was unable to stop, unable to help herself and unable to deny him, no matter what he might ask.

'Tell me. Are you close?'

Close to what? Was there more than this? A release

to this growing tension? Dear God, let it be so, for she would die if she did not…if he did not…

Something.

His hand left her and she moaned at the loss. But he was fumbling with the tie of his robe. It slid off his shoulders, brushing the insides of her calves as it pooled on the bench between them.

She stared down at his naked body, hard muscle, smooth skin, hair, and the mysterious difference between them, hard and long, jutting towards her. She pressed her fingers to herself, trying to ease the sudden, sharp pang of longing. Against all logic, she knew what she wanted him to do and she spread her legs in invitation.

He grabbed the neck of her shift in his hands and ripped it to the hem, taking her bare breasts in his hands before smoothing them down her body as if he was claiming every inch of her. Then he stood and moved towards her.

At the first touch of his body against hers, something inside her seemed to break free, coursing through her blood and wiping all thought from her mind. It was good, whatever it was, and she felt the push and the slight pain as he came into her, but it was lost in the uncontrollable pleasure. He was moving in her and her body was holding, clasping, grasping, trying to take every bit of him in as if she could hold him for ever.

His teeth were at her throat, and his hands on her back as he thrust with barely contained fury. Her breasts were pressed to his chest and she could feel each breath he took, each beat of his heart as if he was a part of her.

'Scream, if you want,' he said, catching her gaze and holding it. 'I will not stop. Not until you break again.'

A shudder went through her, and another. Then a feeling of such longing that words could not express it. Her spirit seemed to leave her body and come crashing back.

As the pleasure took her, she did not scream, as he suggested. Instead, she babbled as if she had been called to make her vows to him again. She begged him to use her, to take her, to do anything he wished with her, so long as this feeling did not end.

She felt him tense in response, so she braced herself against the table and moved her hips against him, urging him on. The pace increased. His breathing became erratic. Then he lost control in a rush, falling still against her and pressing another kiss against her neck. 'Minx,' he whispered. 'Vixen. Temptress.' His nails raked down her back, just hard enough to make her shiver. 'To think you might have wasted such talent staring at the ceiling in the bedroom of some honour-bound prig. It is fortunate for both of us that I ruined your future, for it means I will get to ruin the rest of you at my leisure.'

He sounded very wicked and it made her shiver again. But when he raised his head so she could see his face, he looked different. Younger, less polished, more vulnerable than he had this morning, as if he had shared some part of himself he could not take back.

She gathered her wits and smiled at him. 'You talk much more in the bedroom than you do out of it.' She reached up to brush the loose hair out of her face.

He laughed and tossed his own head as well. 'Then we must do something that will keep me too busy to speak. Let us retire to the bed, Your Grace. Give me a few minutes to regain my strength and we will begin again.'

Chapter Seven

It was dawn when he left her bed, sliding his arm carefully out from under her sleeping body and going to his room. He had dozed as well, exhausted from an extremely satisfying night.

She had been everything he had imagined. Sweet and innocent but surprisingly brave. She must have been terrified to be alone with a man who was a virtual stranger to her, forced by convention to submit to his desires. It was amazing that she had not slammed the door in his face at his first appearance.

Of course, he'd been in such a state after supper that he might have kicked it down had she tried. He did not think of himself as a ravisher of women. He had never needed to be. But this one?

He had held her as an object of desire for so long that he did not trust himself. She had represented all that was forbidden to him. Yet now she was all his.

After seducing her at the dressing table, he'd taken

her to bed for a leisurely session of love play, acquainting her with the pleasures of the flesh and the joy of coupling in various positions, bringing her to climax over and over, until she had finally pleaded with him to stop, curling up in his arms like a satisfied kitten and smiling in her sleep.

He had never been anyone's first lover, and her honesty was so raw and new that he did not know how to respond to it. She was far too inexperienced to play the coquette and lie about her responses. She had enjoyed being with him and would welcome him back to her bed, tonight.

But none of that prepared him for today. He was not used to spending more than a few hours with a woman, much less an entire night. He even avoided the semi-permanent attachments some men entered into, unwilling to reveal the contents of his heart or his head to a mistress paid to lie to him about his character. He preferred his lovemaking to be short and anonymous, where he could leave knowing no more about the women involved than they knew about him.

What was he to do with a woman who would not go away for the rest of his life? A randy part of him wanted a wash and a shave and a return to bed. But she was inexperienced and would probably regret last night's exuberance once the sun rose and her muscles had rested for a bit. He had a lifetime to bed her, there was no rush.

But with the knowledge of all that time, the fear returned. What had he been thinking, taking a wife at all? When they met again, across the breakfast table, what would they have to talk about? He had no trouble making risqué remarks or superficial talk about the weather. But such topics would wear thin in less than a week, and she would still be here, staring at him with those wonderful golden eyes, expecting him to be worthy of his place in society and in her life. If he was not careful, she would see how little substance there was to the man she had married, and the admiration she had given him yesterday would disappear.

He could put off the inevitable for a few hours, at least. She was still asleep, and he was surprisingly alert. So, he summoned his valet for a wash, a shave and a change into his day clothes, then breakfasted and left the house before she could come downstairs.

Once he was outside, he sucked in a breath of cool air and picked up his pace, telling himself that it was nothing more than brisk exercise he needed. He was not running away. He was simply giving her space so she did not tire of him before he did of her.

When Portia awoke, it was almost ten o'clock in the morning, and far later than she usually slept. But after the night she'd had, it was hardly a surprise. It had been almost dawn when she'd finally closed her eyes, too exhausted to do anything but rest in her lover's arms.

She glanced at the empty bed beside her, feeling vaguely disappointed. She had not really expected him to stay with her until morning. All the same, it would have been nice if he had. She wrapped her arms around herself, hugging her shoulders. It was a pale imitation of the way Julian had held her, but it eased the loneliness somewhat.

But not the stiffness, she decided. When Rose arrived, offering to draw her a bath, she accepted eagerly. The maid brought breakfast to her room as well, informing her that His Grace was already gone for the day and had given no notice of when he planned to return.

Was it to be like this every day, she wondered? When she had first come to him, she had promised not to care. But she did, at least a little. There was so much she wanted to ask him, about himself: his likes, his dislikes, his plans for the future. It was strange to know someone so well, to have seen them unclothed and been as close as two people could be, and yet to still be strangers.

So far, she liked him far better than she'd expected to. He had been distant during their earlier meetings, and the standoffishness had continued during the wedding and breakfast. After all her mother's talk about the heartlessness of rakes, she had expected the wedding night to be more nightmare than dream. But he had been surprisingly patient with her. And, as he had promised, she had liked what they'd done together.

More than liked. There were no words for what she felt when she thought of it. She smiled all through bath and breakfast and could not help giggling with Rose, who was looking at her as if they now shared a secret.

At last, she came downstairs and was left with the same challenge she'd had yesterday: how she was to spend her days now that she was the Duchess of Septon. She consulted with Mrs Gates and the cook, only to find that menus for the week were already set. A review of the household accounts proved that groceries had been ordered and bills paid. Things had been running for years without the help of a mistress and could continue on just fine without her input.

'Perhaps a trip to Bond Street,' Mrs Gates suggested.

'Perhaps,' Portia agreed, although she could not think of a thing that she needed. And a shopping trip brought up another problem that she had not considered. 'But if I were to go shopping, I would need money, and I have none.'

Mrs Gates gave her a doubtful look, as if she could

not quite imagine the lady of the house being short of funds. Then she rang for Banks and explained the situation to him.

The butler gave Portia another of his cryptic looks and said, 'His Grace has left no instruction as to what is to be done in this circumstance.' He continued to stare, as if waiting for her apology.

She stared back at him, considering. If she ordered him to obey, what was she to do if he refused? There would be no controlling the staff at all if she allowed the major domo to ignore her requests. 'Has His Grace given you permission to access funds in the house in case of an emergency?' she said, testing the boundaries of his orders.

'There is a cash-box kept in the study that I hold a key to,' he said. There was a faint light of approval in his eyes, and his chin lowered a fraction of an inch as if encouraging her to go on.

'Then I should think the Duke having forgotten to give me an allowance of some kind was an oversight that could constitute such an emergency. It would be very embarrassing, should I run into friends while out and lack the money to buy a Chelsea bun and a cup of tea. Please open the cash-box for me, so that I may go shopping without incident.'

'Very good, Your Grace.' The butler led her to the study, a room she had never been in before.

As he went to a drawer in the desk, she glanced around her, trying to gather as much information as she could about the man who normally inhabited the room. It was tidy, she noted, which said something about her husband, as well as the servants. The top of the desk was clear, save for a book of poetry, the reader's place marked with a scrap of paper.

She had not imagined that Septon had a taste for poems. She'd not imagined him reading at all. Listening to her mother's rants about the foul nature of rakes, she'd assumed they had time for nothing but sin. But even a wicked man must rest sometime, and it seemed her husband found solace in books.

She turned her attention to Banks, who had lifted a small metal box from a drawer and set it on the desk. He unlocked it and stepped back so she might access the contents.

She looked down and struggled to contain her shock. It contained more money than she'd ever seen at one time, bills stacked in a neat pile on top of a handful of coins. She took the paper money out and counted out four hundred pounds, staring at it for a moment, unsure of what to do.

She did not need much. A pound or two would be sufficient, should she want a snack. Then she remembered her mother, and the sad state of affairs in the Braddock household. Things were even worse now that she'd stolen Rose and the house was short a servant.

It was clear that Septon had no such financial problems if he could keep this much money in his desk. She counted out a hundred pounds for herself, tucked it in a pocket of her gown and placed the rest back in the box. Then she smiled at the butler, and said, 'Thank you, Banks. That will be sufficient.'

'Very good, Your Grace,' he replied, his face impassive save for a slight lift at the corner of his lip. 'Shall I call for the carriage?'

'Please,' she said, and went to her room to change.

When she came down, a short time later, the carriage was waiting for her, and liveried servants helped her to her seat. When the driver enquired as to their destination, she paused in confusion. What was she seeking, other than diversion?

She was not accustomed to having money for frivolous purchases. Truly, she did not need anything. Her wardrobe was just as full as it had been when her mother had tried to bully her into a new wedding gown.

After a moment's thought, she said, 'Hatchard's.' In her opinion, one could never have too many books. She certainly could not. When funds had got tight, Mother had been forced to let their subscription to the circulating library lapse, and it had been some time since Portia had been able to read anything but the small selection of books they'd had at home.

Now, if she wished, she could buy as many as she could carry. Even more than that, for she had a groom to carry her packages. She allowed herself to be handed up into the carriage and rode in excited silence to the bookstore, where she passed a pleasurable hour browsing and came away with a stack of novels that would take at least a month to read.

Perhaps the clerk recognised the crest on her carriage door, when it stopped outside the shop, for he was quick to assist her, calling her 'Your Grace' and asking if she wanted the purchases added to her husband's account.

It was an interesting question. She certainly had the funds necessary to pay. But if Julian had a line of credit here, she doubted he would mind, or even notice if she used it. She nodded and watched as the clerk recorded the total in a ledger, then wrapped the books in brown paper for her to take away.

She went back to the carriage and asked the driver to take her to her mother's house. After the scene she had made yesterday, Portia was eager to show her that all was well, and that things were going exactly to plan.

When the housekeeper let her into the parlour, her mother rose and embraced her, smiling. 'You have come to your senses, just as I hoped you would. Have the servants return your clothing to your room, and we will forget this ever happened.'

Portia pulled away from her, holding her at arm's length. 'Do not be silly, Mother. I am only calling to be sure that you are well.'

'Of course I am well. Why would I not be?' her mother replied, giving the same arch look she had used when Portia had worried about her in the past.

'Of course you are,' Portia said to keep the peace. 'But it does my heart good to know for sure. I know you have had money troubles, since Father died. But now that I am married, I can be of help to you.'

'Married to Septon,' her mother said, with a shake of her head to show that she still disapproved. 'How is he treating you, now that you have trapped him?'

'Julian was not trapped by me,' Portia said in a warning tone. 'And he has been treating me very well, thank you.' She hoped she was not blushing, for there was no way to explain how her supposedly wayward husband had behaved, once they were alone together.

If he was avoiding her company during the days, she suspected it was far from unusual behaviour.

'Even a wolf can act like a lamb for one day,' her mother said in a dire voice. 'You will not be so happy with your Julian when he abandons you for an opera dancer.'

'I do quite well on my own,' she said, trying not to brood on the thought. 'And I can always enjoy the company of a good book. He has an account at Hatchard's that I have already made free with. I will lend you the latest novels, once I am through with them.'

Her mother gave a humph of disapproval. 'You would do better to put your money in jewels,' her mother said. 'Make him give you things that are not part of the entail. When it is over, at least you will have something you can sell.'

'Over?' Portia said with a laugh. 'It is only just begun.'

'It is never too soon to plan for your future,' her mother warned. It is wise to have a source of income that he cannot control. Jewels are good for that.'

'Perhaps so,' she said, thinking of her mother's empty jewel case and the brooches and necklaces that she'd sold, since the funeral. 'But I have something even better than that.' She reached into her reticule and removed the stack of bills.

Her mother could not contain her gasp at the sight of the money that Portia placed between them. 'At least the fellow has blunt,' she said, still unsmiling.

Portia took ten pounds back for herself, and handed the rest to her mother. 'This is a wedding gift, from us to you.' It was a lie. But there could be no harm in it if it improved her mother's view of the Duke. 'It should be enough to cover the bills for my come out and the household expenses.'

'More than enough,' her mother admitted.

'Have the cook buy a nice leg of lamb,' Portia coaxed. 'It was always your favourite and you have not had it in ever so long.'

'Or beef,' her mother said, staring at the money. 'A roast would not go amiss.'

Portia patted her arm. 'There, you see. It will not be so bad having me married and away. I can visit you any time you like.'

'And I, you,' her mother said, smiling.

'But not for a while,' Portia said, thinking of her husband's words the previous day. 'Give us time to settle into married life first.'

Her mother gave her another suspicious look. 'You really think he will fall into the role of dutiful husband?'

'I think we are still getting to know each other's habits,' she said, which was a partial truth. She had no idea what life with the Duke would be like in the future. But at the moment, she could not have her mother interfering with it. 'Once we are used to each other, I will certainly invite you to dine with us. Until that time, if you need me for anything, write a note and I will come immediately.' She gave her mother another pat on the arm. 'I must be going now, for it is getting late. But I will come back soon, and we will have a proper visit.'

'I would like that,' her mother said, laying her hand on the money and drawing it towards her as if afraid it might disappear.

'I will give Julian your thanks,' Portia said, since it appeared that her mother did not mean to offer them. Then she went back to the carriage and told the driver to take her home.

Chapter Eight

When Julian returned home after another wasted day, he found his wife sitting in the main salon, absorbed in a book.

She was wearing a rose muslin gown with too many ruffles, and her legs were tucked up under the skirt in a delightfully casual posture. It put him in mind of a bon-bon in a candy shop window, waiting to be unwrapped and enjoyed. And that made him think of welcoming flesh, and bed.

But it was not even dinner time, and she was probably tired and sore from what they had done already. If he had a lifetime to enjoy her, he could at least wait until after the evening meal.

She noticed him standing in the doorway, looking up with a smile as if she was truly glad to see him.

It was disconcerting. He was used to the polite expressions of servants, and Bank's flat voiced greetings that seemed to skirt the line between honour and insolence. How was he to respond to this beautiful stranger, beaming at him as if she'd been waiting all day to see him walk through the door?

'It is a fine day, is it not?' she said.

'I...' He had not noticed. He glanced out the window at the fading sunshine. 'It is indeed.'

'I went out,' she supplied. 'Shopping. It seemed a shame not to enjoy it. Banks ordered the carriage for me.'

Was he supposed to tell her how he'd spent his day? She had promised not to enquire, but what harm would it do? And why was it so difficult to talk to her? He felt naked before her, but there was no reason for it. He cleared his throat, buying time. 'I walked,' he said, feeling like an idiot. If she had the carriage, she must know that he was on foot. 'And went to my club.'

She nodded, politely, still smiling at him.

'Banks gave me some money from the box in your study,' she said, her smile fading slightly. 'I hope you do not mind. I had none of my own, and you did not say anything about an allowance or a household account.'

Money.

Her expression was the epitome of innocence, but the words brought his head down out of the clouds. Money was the real reason she had married him. Money and power. Of course, she was glad to see him, she was already enjoying his largesse without even waiting for permission. 'Mind?' he said, his blood cooling. 'I expected as much from you.'

She looked puzzled for a moment, and then relieved. 'That is good to know. I did not want to act out of turn.'

'There is nothing you could do that would surprise me,' he replied, and gave her a sarcastic smile.

She looked puzzled again, sensing the change in his mood. 'You do not spend much time at home during the day. And you left no instruction,' she reminded him.

'Instruction as to what?' he asked, staring at her.

'My duties, as your wife,' she said, looking at him expectantly.

'You seemed to be able to understand me well enough last night,' he said, and watched her blush. It felt good to shock her, somewhere deep in the black pit that was his heart. But what he'd said was true enough. She had pleased him in the only way that mattered.

'My other duties,' she said in a whisper, as if she was afraid that someone might hear them and realise what she had done with him. 'I assume you wish me to manage the household accounts, and there is the matter of meeting my own expenses.'

'You saw to the last yourself,' he reminded her. 'How much did you take from me?'

'One hundred pounds,' she said in a small voice.

'Impressive,' he said. She was a greedy little thing. He should have guessed as much.

'I will not need any more for quite some time,' she added hurriedly and changed the subject. 'And I asked Mrs Gates to show me the household accounts. They are all in good order.'

'Then it appears that you do not need my input at all,' he said, turning to leave her.

'There is one other matter,' she said cautiously. 'An invitation came in the afternoon post. The Duchess of Belleville is having a ball and has invited us.' She gave him a significant look and added, 'Both of us. You have said nothing about wishing to go about in public as a couple.'

Was she so ashamed of him that she had to ask? In his fantasies, he had occasionally imagined the two of them dancing, when he was not thinking of other things far more sordid. In those dreams, she would be looking up at him adoringly, and not as she was now, as if the prospect of being seen with him made her thoroughly uncomfortable. 'That was assumed,' he said dryly. 'Since I married you.'

'Well…yes. But I did not wish to accept anything without consulting you.' She stared at him nervously.

'How kind,' he said, watching her closely. If she did not want to go about with him, then Honoria Redmond was just the person he wanted her to meet. 'The Duchess of Belleville? By all means, accept. She is an old friend and is probably eager to meet you.'

She smiled at him again, clearly relieved that they had come to an agreement. 'I will write out an acceptance, immediately,' she said.

'And next, I suppose you will tell me that you have nothing to wear,' he said, waiting for the bargaining that had always followed the arrival of such an invitation, when his mother and father had received one.

She looked baffled for a moment, then said, 'On the contrary, I am sure I have something that will suit. I purchased a new wardrobe at the beginning of the Season.'

'But that was before you became a duchess,' he reminded her, waiting for her denials to become demands.

'True,' she agreed. 'But the gowns I have are quite lovely.'

'Are you sure?' he said. 'You have taken more than enough money to buy a gown. Go and do so. You will want to look your best.'

'Why?' she asked.

'Your appearance will reflect on me,' he said, making the case for her since she was slow to do it for herself.

'And you care so much about your reputation,' she said pointedly, turning the argument back onto him.

'In some cases, yes,' he admitted. 'If I am to become a staid, married man, I want the world to know I have done it for a good reason.'

'Other than to polish away the tarnish of the duel and keep the Crown from having you up on charges?' Her parry was surprisingly blunt, and he could not help but smile.

'Well, yes, there is that, of course,' he said. 'But, to prove that you are happy and are not bothered by my past, I wish you to shine on our first outing together. I assume that will require a new ball gown and all that accompanies it. And jewels,' he added, staring at her bare throat. 'I think I shall buy you a wedding gift.'

'You do not have to,' she said, giving him a suspicious look.

'I think I do,' he said. If he did not, she would likely tell someone he hadn't bothered. It was best not to give her ammunition to use against him. 'Topaz, I think. It is not as valuable as some stones, but it will bring out the colour of your eyes.'

'I am surprised you've noticed,' she said, looking away and blushing again.

'I notice everything about you,' he admitted. 'Your eyes, your hair, the angle of your shoulder as it slopes to your breast.' The honesty of it embarrassed him.

But she was lovely, sitting there, with the fading sunlight bringing out the gold in her hair and shining off the tips of her lashes. 'In time, I will know you better than you do yourself.'

'Will I know you as well?' she whispered without looking up.

'You already know everything you need to,' he said. 'I am what I am, and you had best get used to it.' He turned to go. 'I will see you at dinner.'

'Until then,' she said, and he felt her eyes on him as he left the room.

Later, as she dressed for dinner, Portia thought back to the conversation with Julian, trying to decide when it had gone wrong. She suspected it was when she had told him of the money she'd taken. But he had left her with nothing. What else was she supposed to do?

The answers to that were obvious. She could have waited until he'd returned and asked him. She could have taken less. She could have told him yesterday of her mother's urgent need of assistance.

Well, perhaps not that last. She would have to explain eventually. But the way her mother was behaving, it would be better if the two of them forgot each other, at least for a few days.

But how was she to explain that she no longer had enough money to buy the sort of gown he wished her to get? She'd had no plans to shop when she'd given the money to her mother, this afternoon. Ten pounds could be stretched to last for months if she was careful. But apparently, duchesses were not supposed to be frugal.

As she walked down the stairs to the dining room, she forced the question to the back of her mind. It was never a good idea to speak of money over dinner, especially if she wished to keep her husband in a good humour.

When she sat down at the table, he was already there, sipping his wine. He glanced in her direction, drained the glass and signalled for it to be refilled as if he sought strength in alcohol.

Apparently, it would take some effort to regain his trust. She smiled and cocked her head towards the hall as the long case clock chimed eight. 'I am not late, am I?'

'Obviously not,' he said, tipping his head as she had done.

She nodded and smiled as the footmen brought the soup and Julian filled her bowl, feeling like a mechanical doll with a painted-on happiness that could not be changed. She took her first spoonful and was about to proclaim it delicious when she saw the jaded look on his face.

It was fine soup. He knew. He knew she knew. There was no need to speak of it.

They continued to eat in silence.

'I went to Hatchard's, today,' she blurted, when she could no longer stand the quiet.

'A bookstore,' he said, as if it surprised him.

'Yes,' she said, looking down into her soup. 'I enjoy reading, very much.'

'Hmm,' he said, going back to his soup. It was not much of a response, but at least it was not openly hostile.

'When I realised that I had nothing to do this afternoon, I could not resist the opportunity. I bought several new books.'

Then she remembered the rest of the transaction and her words slowed. 'But... When I tried to pay... They said they would put the bill on your account. Is that all right?' She held her breath and waited for his response, sure that it would result in another frosty comment.

He stared at her for a moment as if he could not quite figure out what to do with her. Then he shook his head and pushed the soup bowl away, signalling for the next course to be brought. At last, he spoke. 'There are worse ways to spend my money than on books. I suppose it is too much to hope that you have purchased a history or some other such edifying topic.'

She shook her head, sadly. 'Novels only, I'm afraid. Gothic romances. I am sure you will find them all quite horrible.'

His lip twitched and for a moment, she suspected he was about to laugh. Then his composure returned. 'Terrible, indeed.'

'I got you Lord Byron's latest collection of poems, as well,' she added.

'Whatever possessed you…' He was staring at her with surprise, but there was no anger in it. He looked changed, as he had last night, after they'd made love. It was as if she had caught him naked and left him struggling to cover things he normally kept hidden.

'When Banks took me into the study to get the money, I saw the book on your desk,' she said with a shrug.

'That would explain it,' he said, relaxing again and sampling the meat on his plate.

'If you leave it in the drawing room when you are finished with it, I would like to read it as well,' she said.

'It is not a novel,' he reminded her.

'I read poetry on occasion,' she said. 'Perhaps we could discuss it, some night.'

'Perhaps,' he said, and went back to his meal.

Silence fell again.

She ate her beef and pondered her next move. It

was as if a door had opened briefly, then shut again, leaving her on the wrong side. What could she say that would prop it open for a longer time? After much searching, she found a topic that would interest them both. 'May I ask you something?'

He did not look up, but said, 'What would you like to know?'

'Can you tell me about my father? He was a friend of yours, was he not?'

'He was.' He looked up and then down again, as if the topic was a difficult one. 'One of my best friends.'

'What was he like?' she said, holding her breath as she waited for the answer.

'Surely, you knew him better than I,' Julian said, avoiding the question.

She shook her head. 'He was rarely home, and when he was, he never spoke to me about anything important.'

'He spoke *of* you, often,' His gaze rose slowly to hers, and he looked at her as he had on the previous evening, as if he never wanted to look away.

'What did he say?' She leaned forward in her seat, more eager for this answer than she had realised she was.

Now Julian was looking at her with sympathy. 'He praised your intelligence and your beauty. He said you were very like your mother, who he loved as well.'

'And yet, he argued with her, nearly every time he was home,' she said, amazed.

'Some men are better off if they do not marry,' he said slowly, and she wondered if he also spoke of himself. 'My own father…' he began, and then stopped again and shook his head. 'It is your father you wished to hear of. He was a man of many excesses. But beneath them all, he had a good and loyal heart.'

'To his friends, perhaps,' she said, and watched as her husband winced. 'What was he like when he was with you?'

'He had a sharp mind and a wicked sense of humour,' Julian said, remembering his friend. 'No one could beat him at chess, for he seemed to see the whole game in a single move.'

'On the few nights he was home, he taught me both chess and cards.' She smiled fondly, remembering. 'Mother did not approve of gambling, but he said it was more fun to play for a penny a point and he often let me win. It was how I got my spending money.'

'That sounds very like him,' Julian said, then looked at her strangely. 'Except for him letting you win. He would never have turned you loose on the world after giving you a false sense of your own abilities. There is nothing more dangerous than an overconfident gambler.'

'Judging by the debts he left us with, that was probably true,' she said, shaking her head.

'He was a masterful card player, when he was sober,' Julian said. 'But he had a weakness for drink. He could never leave a bottle half-full. I tried to dissuade him, but there was nothing I could do.'

'Thank you for kindness in trying,' she said, attempting to hide the sadness she still felt when she thought of her father's last days. She looked at Julian, considering. 'I wonder if he would have been surprised that you married me?'

'He would have been horrified,' her husband said, a little too quickly. It made her wonder if he felt the same.

'I think, perhaps not. He was fond of you,' she said firmly and watched as his features relaxed. 'He would not have asked you to watch over me if he had not believed you had many admirable qualities.'

He thought for a moment, then shook his head. 'It is not for me to decide what virtues he might have seen in me, and unfortunately, he is not here to explain himself.'

'I am sure I will understand in time.' She smiled at him.

He took another bite of his dinner, turning his attention to the next course as if to signal his desire that the conversation might end.

But for her, it was far from over. 'And this guardianship. What did you think of it?'

'What did I think?' He looked up at her with something very like panic before schooling his face into the usual, impassive mask. 'I did not like it,' he said. 'I was counting the days until you married so I could be free of it.' He gave her a cold smile as if it gave him pleasure to hurt her.

She smiled back, refusing to give him the satisfaction of seeing her pain. 'It must be very disappointing to find yourself trapped with me for life, then.'

'I do not regret marrying you,' he said in a softer tone and reached out to take her hand, resting his thumb against the pulse in her wrist. 'In some ways, it has been surprisingly pleasant.'

She didn't pull away, and let her hand rest passively in his. But by the light that shone in his eyes, she was sure he could feel her heart beat faster at the thought of what they might do together, once dinner was over. 'And you,' he said in a seductive whisper. 'Do you regret marrying me?'

She let out a nervous laugh. 'Of course not. You have been very…' Was she about to say *kind*? For they both knew he had not been. She began again. 'You made me a duchess. I have more than I ever hoped for. Why should I not be happy?'

'Why, indeed?' He was looking at her as if he wondered who she was trying to convince. Then he signalled for the dessert course to be brought. 'After dinner, I will take my port in the sitting room, and you can show me the books you have bought.'

'I would like that,' she said, trying to relax again, as the footman brought out an elegantly moulded muscadine ice. When they had finished it, she went to the library and brought her purchases to him, setting them on a table next to his chair and taking a seat on the other side of it. She picked a book from the top of the stack after offering him his volume of poetry and settled down to read.

Normally, it took only moments to become so absorbed in a story that she forgot the world around her. But with him beside her, it was impossible to concentrate. She found herself stealing glances at him, wondering what he thought of her gift.

She wondered as well what would happen when they grew tired of reading. Would he come to her room as he had last night? Just the thought of it made her warm in a way that the fire in front of them did not.

He began to read aloud, slowly and with feeling. His voice was deep, velvety and beautiful, another kind of seduction. The book she had been reading slipped from her hands, forgotten as she lost herself in the sound of him.

He stopped and looked up, smiling. 'Have you tried port, my dear?'

She blinked in surprise. 'Certainly not.'

He took a sip from his glass and turned it towards her, offering her the place where his lips had touched. 'Tonight, you shall.'

Hesitantly, she took the glass, warming it in her hands. She sipped as he began to read again. The wine was thick and sinfully rich, an excellent match for the heady words read in his seductive voice. She closed her eyes and sipped again, letting the words wash over her.

'*"And all that's best of dark and bright Meet in her aspect and her eyes..."*' He stopped reading and she opened her eyes again to find him watching her intently.

'It is a lovely poem,' she murmured.

'Yes,' he said. 'Lovely.' Then he set the book aside and touched her hand as if he had not been talking about poetry at all. 'That is enough for tonight, I think. It is time for bed.'

'We could take the book with us,' she said, surprising herself. It was probably the wine talking. She had never been so forward in her life.

He smiled and tucked the book in his pocket before taking her hand and leading her towards the stairs.

Chapter Nine

They had been married five days. Each day, he had left the house after breakfast, marking time until dinner when he could come home to her. And each night they had made love. She was coming to know him, responding to his likes and dislikes and timidly expressing her own. It had been a delightful week, and she had been everything he'd imagined she might be in those long months before the duel.

It could not last.

Nothing good ever did. It had been years since he'd spent so many nights in a row at home. It would be wise of him to go out in the evening, as he used to, just to remind them both that she was not the only thing in his life. She had promised, when she'd first come to him, that his comings and goings would not matter to her. It was time he put that promise to the test.

And it was Wednesday, after all. He had plans for

dinner that did not include her, and he had no intention of changing them. He left her, asleep and exhausted in her own bed and dozed in his own for a few hours before summoning his valet to prepare him for the day.

He went downstairs for a hurried breakfast. At his instruction, the cook prepared the usual Wednesday basket of dainties, and Banks went down to the wine cellar for a bottle of champagne that would match with it. Then he informed the butler that he would be home late, as he always was on Wednesdays.

'Is Her Grace aware of your plans?' the butler said, showing far more curiosity than was appropriate.

Julian stared back at him, refusing to feel the guilt that the old retainer was trying to inflict on him. 'She is still asleep. Inform her when she comes down to breakfast that she should not expect me for supper.'

'Very good, Your Grace,' he replied in a tone that belied his words.

'Thank you for your support, Banks,' Julian said, returning the butler's sour look. Then he picked up the wine and basket and left the house.

When Portia came down to breakfast, it was almost ten o'clock. But after the night they'd had, she could hardly be blamed for rising late. She wondered how Julian managed on so little sleep, for he was always out of the house and gone for hours when she managed to drag herself from bed. Did he nap at his club, she wondered? The man did not seem to need sleep at all.

It was far from the only mystery about him, for he rarely spoke of anything when they dined and said even less when they were in bed. She did not think that the poetry she had asked him to recite counted as conversation. The only thing that had revealed was his ability to speak from memory a wide variety of verses, some of which were rather scandalous.

She sat down at the table and smiled as she stirred her tea. It was not even noon, and she was already looking forward to the night that was to come and the sweet hours they would spend together. A week ago, she had thought that she and Julian would live as strangers in the same house and the same bed. She had never imagined what was to come and how quickly her life could change.

From the doorway of the breakfast room, Banks cleared his throat.

She set down her spoon and turned to look at him.

'Your Grace,' he said with a slight bow.

She smiled and gave him a nod of encouragement.

'His Grace requested that I inform you he will not be home for supper.'

'He did?' Her smile faltered and it was a moment before she could regain control and present the untroubled appearance that she wished to. 'Did he say where he was going?'

'I would not presume to ask, Your Grace.'

'Of course not,' she said in a weak voice.

'He is in the habit of dining out on Wednesdays,' the butler supplied, looking as uncomfortable as she felt.

'When does he usually return?' she said, hating herself for wondering.

'It is not part of my duties to monitor his comings and goings,' he said. But the corner of his mouth turned down in an expression of displeasure. It seemed that he did not like his employer's absence any more than she did.

'Thank you for informing me,' she said, picking up her cup and taking a sip of tea. 'That will be all, Banks.' Then she reached for the toast rack as if everything was fine and nothing had changed.

'Very good, Your Grace,' he said, and left her alone again.

She stared at the slice of bread she had placed on her plate, in no mood to eat it. Julian had said nothing about longstanding Wednesday plans when they'd been together last night.

Of course, Julian had said nothing about anything of any real importance. He never did. He'd praised her breasts, comparing them to poems, which she'd found a ridiculous but flattering metaphor. He had made several lewd suggestions of the sort she'd never have imagined a week ago, much less complied with. But he'd not informed her that he would be abandoning her the very next day to go back to his old habits.

She took a deep breath and picked up her knife, buttering her toast with a series of short, uneven strokes. The butter was made from the cream of the Septon Manor dairy. She added marmalade, which she had been assured was made by Cook with fruit taken from the Duke's orangery. There was no point in depriving herself of breakfast, which was as delicious as every other meal from the Septon kitchens.

That was the point of marrying, after all. She had wanted security for herself and her mother and had achieved it. She had sworn to the Duke that she would be the perfect wife, an asset to his holdings, much like the dairy cows and the orange trees. If he chose to miss a meal with her, that was hardly abandonment. Even if it was, she had promised not to pester him about his habits, as long as he held up his half of the bargain and provided for her.

For all she knew, this was a test of her sincerity. What sort of wife would she be if, the very first time he left her alone, she whined and wheedled and complained, all after swearing that she knew his nature and did not care.

She did not care. Today, she would avail herself of

all the luxury her new position offered. Perhaps another trip to Bond Street would make her feel better. She would request a change in the menu for the evening. The salmon that they'd had for the wedding breakfast and apricots for the dessert course. She would spend the evening reading one of her new novels. In no time at all, he would be home again and visiting her room.

The afternoon passed, as did dinner and the evening hours. She prolonged bedtime as long as she could, telling herself that she was absorbed in a book. But at midnight, she was forced to admit that she had been reading the same page over and over for half an hour while listening for the sound of the front door.

She went to bed to continue the vigil in a less obvious place, staring into the darkness of her room, alert for the sounds of movement in the room next to her and the muted voices of master and valet, preparing for bed. But the house was silent and eventually she succumbed to sleep.

When Julian arrived home, it was well past midnight. That was hardly unusual, he reminded himself. Some of his happiest evenings had been spent wandering the streets of London in the wee hours.

Until recently, at least. This week, there had been several memorable nights spent at home, and a few specific instances that ranked amongst his life's happiest memories. He felt a twinge of guilt at the thought of Portia, immediately followed by an unexpected surge of excitement. She was waiting for him.

Well, perhaps not *for him*, specifically. It would not do to imagine her like a spaniel staring out the window, anticipating the return of the master. She had a life and interests of her own to occupy her time and had promised not to interfere in his. All the same, it might be rather nice to have someone who cared where he had been and was eager to see him arrive safe at home.

Someone other than Banks, of course. When he got to the door, the butler was there to let him in, giving him the same pained look he always did, as if wishing his master to the devil for keeping him up, awaiting his homecoming.

Julian smiled back at him, refusing to apologise for his behaviour which, compared to his usual outings, had been quite tame. 'Good evening, Banks.'

'Good morning, Your Grace.' The butler shut the door behind him, clicking the lock into place as if to remind him that it was still too early for decent people to be up and about.

'I don't suppose Her Grace is still up,' he said, glancing down the darkened hall of the ground floor.

'I wouldn't presume to know, Your Grace,' Banks

said with an unflinching stare. Then he added, 'She retired some time ago when she grew tired.'

Of waiting for you.

The butler did not say the words, but the accusation was there, all the same.

'Oh. Well then, I will go to bed as well,' Julian said, making his way to the stairs. As he started up, he did not bother to be quiet about it. When he arrived at his door, he let it swing closed behind him instead of shutting it noiselessly. He stopped to listen for movement from the next room.

There was none. No light shown from the crack beneath the connecting door. He stared at it for a moment, considering. If he wanted her, there was no reason to hint about it. He did not have to wait for an invitation. He could simply open the door and go to her. Wake her, take her, and go to sleep.

He frowned, confused. Wanting a woman to help him ease the last hour before sleep was hardly unusual. But what he had been wishing for just now was a chance to sink into sweet oblivion while lying beside her. How easy would it be to lose himself inside her and then close his eyes and drift, not rising until morning?

He stepped back from the door, alarmed. It was one thing to seek satisfaction from a woman, and quite another to stay with her afterwards. He was not given to embarrassing displays of dependence on anyone and had no plans to become reliant on his new wife.

He pulled off his cravat, which suddenly seemed uncomfortably tight, then shed his coat as well, dropping it on a chair as he walked back to his dressing table to complete the process of undressing. He did not need wife or valet to put himself to bed. He would be fine on his own.

He woke later than usual, tired and foul tempered, in no mood to start the day. It seemed that it was one thing to declare one's independence and quite another to actually enjoy it. He had lain awake in the dark for several hours, listening to the night sounds of the house and thinking of Portia, soft, warm and just a room away. He had fallen into an uneasy sleep just before dawn, only to be up again a few hours later when the servants rose and began their duties.

It served him right for coming home early and still sober. The best way to guarantee a few hours of rest was to make sure that one was thoroughly depleted when one finally lay down. He would know better tonight. If he decided to eschew the marital bed, he would not bother coming home until he was too tired to care about the woman who had not bothered to wait up for him.

She was waiting for him at the breakfast table when

he came downstairs and had the nerve to look surprised when he sat down beside her.

'You are here,' she said, setting down her cup of chocolate and pouring his coffee.

'I live here,' he said, unable to hide his irritation. 'Am I not welcome at breakfast in my own home?'

'Of course you are,' she said, returning to her meal. 'I am simply unaccustomed to see you home at this hour.'

'You hardly know me well enough to predict my schedule,' he said, glaring into his cup and adding far too much sugar.

'I only know what you see fit to inform me,' she said. Her tone was tart, but the accompanying smile was as overly sweet as his coffee. 'But do as you will.'

'I do not need your invitation for that either,' he said, taking a gulp from his cup and refusing to admit his mistake.

'Of course not, Julian,' she said demurely.

He glared at her as he reached for the shirred eggs, wondering how a woman who agreed with everything he said could still be so annoying.

Before he could ask for it, she passed him the toast rack. It was as if she was reading his mind.

He had to resist the urge to growl.

'I went shopping yesterday,' she said, apropos of nothing. 'I am having a gown made for the Duchess of Belleville's ball, as you suggested,' she said. 'I sent the bill to your bank.'

He looked up sharply and found her still staring at him with a placid smile. So why did he feel this was some sort of punishment for not coming home? Possibly because he knew, after her first shopping trip that she had more than enough money to pay for any purchases she might have made.

It was nothing less than he'd expected, when he'd agreed to marry her, this financial game-playing. It should not bother him, for he had the money to cover any debts she might run up. All the same, he was annoyed. He had been gone just one night, and she was already searching for ways to punish him. What would she be like in a month or a year, when he had tired of playing house with her and gone back to the life he enjoyed?

'It will be verdigris green,' she said, oblivious to his mood.

'I suppose that is a hint about the jewels I promised you,' he said, frowning.

'I... No,' she fumbled. 'You do not have to get me anything, if you don't wish to.'

'You would look ridiculous without something around your neck,' he snapped. 'Unfinished.'

'Perhaps so,' she agreed cautiously. 'I have nothing

of my own that would suit. But, if you had some old, family piece…'

'I will do as I promised,' he said, through gritted teeth. 'My word is good.'

'I never doubted it,' she said hurriedly, looking down at her breakfast as if afraid to meet his eye.

If this had been an argument, he had won it. But he felt confusion, rather than satisfaction. All his instincts told him to reach out in comfort to assure her that nothing was wrong. He was simply tired and short tempered. But wasn't that her fault as well?

If she'd not come to him with this mad idea to marry, then he would not be having such strange feelings now. He'd still have been troubled with unfulfillable lust. But that was an understandable urge and nothing like the anger and panic he was feeling right now.

He pushed his eggs away and forced down the last of his too-sweet coffee. Then he rose, taking care not to rush. 'I will not be home for dinner,' he said, and felt a measure of calm returning. Then he added, 'Do not bother to wait up.'

'As you wish, Your Grace,' she said, and went back to her breakfast as if nothing had happened.

When Julian was gone from the dining room, Portia waited a moment until she heard the front door close and was sure he was gone. Then she pushed her plate away, in no mood to eat. Had she done something to offend him? Or was it merely as her mother had said, that rakes took pleasure in breaking hearts?

Perhaps it was her announcement that she had been spending money on a gown. She'd worked her admission of the bill into the conversation as skilfully as she could, hoping he would not notice. But he had seemed angry from the first moment he'd come to the table.

She had not seen him at all yesterday. And yet the night before that, they had parted as lovers. If he was as much of a rake as her mother said he was, he would be out most nights, as her father had been. She should not be surprised about it, for she'd thought when planning for this marriage, that they would not spend much time together.

Of course, at that time, she had not imagined that she would enjoy his company as much as she did. She had done everything possible to make him happy. And yet, he was not. Was he seeking another lover already? Or was it something far more innocent?

She got up from the table and went into the hall, only to see Banks, who relaxed enough to give her a look of pity.

'Where does he go, when he is away?' she said, not bothering to dress the question in subterfuge.

She sighed and held up her hands in defeat. 'I do not know why I bothered to ask. You would not presume to know.'

To her surprise, the butler responded, 'Parliament is in session this afternoon and will run until late in the evening.'

'And if he is gone after that?' she asked.

'I would not presume to know,' Banks said, just as she had predicted. 'But I am told that gentlemen seldom keep secrets from their valets.'

'Thank you, Banks,' she said, smiling. She went upstairs to the bedrooms. In the room next to her, she could hear Mason, the valet, going about his duties.

She opened the door between the rooms, surprising the man, who was standing at the foot of the bed, a stack of freshly laundered shirts in his hands. 'Your Grace?' he said nervously.

'Mason,' she replied, equally nervous.

'Is there something I can assist you with? Should I call your maid?'

'That will not be necessary,' she said, wetting her lips. 'I was simply wondering where His Grace was likely to go after the Parliament session is finished this evening.'

'I don't know if I should...' His voice trailed away.

This was far better than Bank's insistence that he did not know. Mason had information. He just did not wish to share it. She straightened and smiled, reminding herself that she was the mistress of the house and not without power. 'Did he forbid you from telling me?' she asked.

'Well, no,' the servant admitted.

'Is there any reason that his whereabouts need to be secret?' she said. 'A matter of state, perhaps?'

'I do not think so,' he said, his brow furrowing.

'The Duke and I have an agreement,' she said, giving him a conspiratorial wink. 'I will not bother him about his activities, and he will not meddle in mine. There is no reason for either of us to keep secrets.'

'Of course not, Your Grace,' he said obediently.

'And that is why he will not mind if you tell me where he is likely to go,' she said, giving him an expectant look.

'He sometimes favours gaming on Thursdays,' Mason said cautiously.

'And when he does, is there a particular haunt he frequents?' she pressed.

'The Inferno is his favourite,' he admitted, then added, 'You will find the coachman knows the way.'

'Thank you for your help,' she said with a nod. 'There is no reason to speak to the Duke about this discussion.'

'That would be for the best,' he agreed.

She went back to her room and closed the door. The day before her would be long and dull. But the evening could prove quite exciting.

Chapter Ten

That night, after dinner, Portia went to her room and summoned Rose. 'How does one dress to go to a gaming hell?' she asked, staring into the mirror at her reflection. She certainly did not look like the sort of woman who would frequent one. Changes would have to be made.

The maid looked back at her, baffled. 'I do not think ladies go to them at all. Courtesans, perhaps,' she admitted.

'I assume a disguise will be needed,' Portia said. 'Could we make a mask out of some lace? And style my hair in a different way? Perhaps you could hide it under a turban and leave only a few curls showing.'

Rose nodded, considering. 'And you should wear your most risqué gown. There is a red one that you have never worn.'

'It did not suit me, I thought,' she admitted. 'But with a bit of rouge to change my colouring, it might do well.' Rose pulled the gown out of the wardrobe, and they set to work.

When they had finished their preparations, Portia stood back to admire the results in a mirror. She was not quite unrecognisable. But in a darkened room full of strangers who did not expect to meet a duchess, she might go unnoticed. If her husband was there and happened to recognise her, she would claim that she had come for her own purposes. It would be as if she had not broken her word at all. Once she was sure that there was nothing untoward going on, she could go home to sleep.

But what if there was something to see?

She gave herself an encouraging smile. Then it would serve her right, she supposed. Her mother had warned her of the problems she might experience in this marriage, and she had ignored her advice. It was time to see who her husband was when he was not at home, and to make peace with the truth. So, she ordered her maid to summon the carriage and told the coachman to take her to The Inferno.

The coachman gave her a doubtful look but helped her to her seat and drove them through town until they reached St James Street. There, he stopped in front of a windowless building with a black enamelled door. There were no words on the sign hanging above it, just a colourful painting of sinners in a torment of flames.

She hesitated for a moment as the coachman opened the door for her, then said, 'Wait for me, here.'

The driver nodded, pulling to the nearest corner as she walked up to the door and knocked.

It was opened by a burly man in a red coat trimmed in gold braid, who squinted down at her but made no move to step aside. 'What's your business, here, miss?'

She stared up at him. Was there a password of some sort? If there was, she would be turned away on the doorstep. 'Dante sent me,' she said, adjusting her mask to make sure it obscured her features. 'I want to play a game.'

The man laughed and waved her in. 'You are in the right place, I suppose. If you don't belong here, you will have to learn it on your own, soon enough.'

She walked down a long, darkened hallway past closed doors on either side, growing more hesitant with each step, until she reached the back of the house, where another red liveried man waited at a green baize door. The man gave her a dubious look, then opened it and waved her through.

She stopped in the doorway and surveyed the room. The decoration was opulent to an excessive degree, with gilt mirrors and sconces and walls draped with rich red cloth, as if it had been decorated as a poor person thought a rich person's house might look. She had imagined something far more forbidding than this. What waited before her was nothing more than a sham to draw in pigeons for plucking. If she kept her wits about her, there was nothing to fear.

She walked forward, between gaming tables for cards and dice, wheels for EO and the special faro tables, which her father had told her were too easy to rig and never to be trusted.

The majority of the players gathered around them were men, some of whom she recognised from the balls she had attended in the early part of the Season. But tonight, there was an easiness about their manners that had not existed in the more formal events she'd met them at. She caught snatches of conversation as she passed by, cursing, lewd comments and ribald laughter that made her glad of the mask concealing her blushes.

But this was no time to be embarrassed. She was here to find Julian, who must be somewhere in this throng of gamblers. Or, perhaps, it would be easier to let him find her. What better way to do that than to use the skills her father had given her? She reached into her reticule for the ten pounds she'd kept from her husband's money, found an empty card table and signaled the dealer that she wanted to play.

It was a night like many others. Parliament had adjourned at nine, and then he'd dined at his club and come to The Inferno to finish the evening with cribbage and brandy. The liquor was good and luck was with him. He would be leaving with more money than he'd brought.

Julian had never been so bored in his life.

He reached into his waistcoat pocket and fished out his watch to check the time. Only midnight and hours left before he usually went home.

'Not betting the watch, are you?' said the man across the table from him.

'No need,' Julian said, indicating the pile of coins in front of him.

'Then keep your mind on the game,' the other snapped, counting out his hand and moving his peg around the board.

Julian dropped the watch back in his pocket and counted his points as well. Maybe the fellow was right. It was never a good idea to gamble when one's mind was not sharp. Tonight his thoughts were at home with his wife. Was she asleep, he wondered? Or reading one of her books by the sitting room fire. Was she thinking about him at all?

If she was, was she longing for his return or dreading it? He'd been an ass at breakfast. Perhaps she had married him only for his money. But he had married her to gain access to her body. Now he was denying himself to prove some sort of point, which would not hurt her in the least. A sensible man would go home to her bed. What they did there was surely worth the price of a ball gown or two.

How long did he mean to waste here before he gave up and admitted defeat? Usually he played until the sun rose and enjoyed the time. But tonight it was a struggle even to finish the current game. He tossed his cards down and prepared to collect his winnings.

Then he heard a stir at the doorway of the club and the surprised mutterings of the men around him. He looked up to find the source of the disturbance. Suddenly, the night changed from excruciatingly common to a novel delight.

The mask did nothing to disguise the woman standing in the doorway, at least not to him. The red dress was strange, and the turban might hide her hair, but he recognised her immediately all the same. He knew the slight sway of her hips, the way her breasts rose and fell as she walked, the way she bit her lip as she considered the entertainments before her and the honey-coloured eyes peeping from behind the lace that covered her face. After a year and a half of longing and a few days of possession, every element of her being was as familiar to him as the lines on his own hand.

A decent husband would grab his wife and take her from this place at once, to spare her from the ogling eyes of the drunken men around her. At the very least he should make sure that the generous allowance she had taken from him would not be fleeced from her as if she were an innocent lamb at shearing.

But he was not that sort of man. He wanted to see what she meant to do, now that she was here. She had come after him, he was sure, for he had never seen her here before. In a week's time she had turned his own servants against him, and they'd betrayed his location so that she could follow him and drag him home like a recalcitrant child.

It was clever of her, and foolish of him. He should have left instructions not to reveal his plans. He had never strictly forbidden them from telling their new mistress about his habits. He had never thought she would care enough to ask. He could not decide whether to be impressed or annoyed.

But as he looked at her, he could not help smiling. She was doing nothing as yet to interfere with his play. Nothing, except existing in the same space he occupied. Hadn't that always been enough to drive him to distraction?

As he watched, she took a seat at a piquet table, opposite a young lord who had courted her earlier in the Season. Seeing them together, Julian felt the same spike of jealousy that he'd felt the last time he'd watched them talking, the desire to barge into the conversation and force her to acknowledge him.

It was not necessary to make a scene. They were married. She would be going home with him. The thought moved in him like a low fire, turning the old, hollow yearning into anticipation. He took his drink and left his table to watch her play.

As the game began, she showed no sign of discomfort at the unwelcoming surroundings. She bet as if she was in her own drawing room, playing for buttons instead of pounds. Her hands on the cards were mesmerising, the motions elegant as she shuffled and dealt, then arranged the cards in front of her. Her moves as she laid them down were quick, concise and sure.

Julian moved to stand behind her opponent, but she gave no indication that she recognised him, remaining focused on the game in progress, her face giving away no secrets. In no time, she defeated the fellow, taking ten pounds off him without losing her smile.

He had never been so aroused.

Perhaps it was the way she nibbled her lip as she considered her play that drove him near to madness. Or perhaps it was the way she was ignoring him. But seeing her here was like seeing her for the first time, all over again. He wanted to be shuffled and dealt, used and discarded. He wanted to lie down on the table and let her work her magic on him until the sun rose.

Was her opponent similarly distracted, or was it simply her skill that bested him? For she was simply that good, every bit as sharp as her father had been at his best. After several games, and an equal number of losses, the man she had challenged pushed away from the table with a shake of his head.

The minute the chair was empty, Julian took his place.

They stared at each other for a moment in silence, and her smile never wavered. Then she said, 'Fancy a game, Your Grace?'

'Do you enjoy games?' he asked, smiling back at her.

'I would not be here if I did not,' she said, shuffling the cards, dealing and laying out the talon between them.

'What shall we wager?' he asked.

'That is up to you, I think,' she said.

He smiled. 'It is never wise to let your opponent have such power over you, especially when he is a man and you are a desirable young woman.'

'Perhaps I am just that confident in my play,' she said teasingly.

He laughed. 'Then we will play for your honour.'

'Do you often make such wagers?' she said, tipping her head to the side and biting her lip again.

'Only on very special occasions,' he said, 'with very special women.'

'And I am special?' she said with a faint smile.

'Very.'

'Then I accept the challenge. But what will you give me if I win?'

'Whatever you wish,' he said, thinking that the results would be the same either way.

Her mask twitched as she raised her eyebrows. 'That is a dangerous wager as well,' she replied, and finished dealing.

Play began, and he was surprised to find it difficult to gain points against her. She exchanged cards like a master declaring carte blanche on more than one of the deals. At the end of the game, she had beaten him just as easily as she had the last player.

He set his hand down with a wry smile and held his hands out to her as if waiting to be manacled. 'It seems I am at your mercy.'

She responded with a slow, bedroom smile that heated his blood and quickened his pulse. 'So it seems.'

'What do you wish from me?'

She glanced around them. 'Nothing you could forfeit here.'

'I will escort you home, where we can discuss it further,' he said, rising and offering her his hand.

'I have a carriage waiting outside,' she said.

His carriage. He had not bothered with it tonight, for he preferred his morning walks home and the strange, exhausted peace they brought after a long night's entertainment. The sensation of riding with Portia, seated just across from him, was soothing as well. It was not the first time he had found comfort in a woman after a night of gambling. But those had been empty pleasures compared to this strange seduction.

'Why did you come out tonight?' he asked, staring at her, fascinated by the way the light and shadow played on her masked face as they rode through the night.

'Why did you?' she asked, staring back.

'I sought diversion,' he said. But what did he wish to be diverted from? Not her. Perhaps it was the noise of his own thoughts that kept him always searching for distraction.

'I wanted to see what it was like, where you were,' she said.

'I thought you promised you would not question my comings and goings,' he said, trying to turn the tables on her.

'I did nothing to prevent you,' she reminded him. 'You did not have to sit down to play with me, nor did you have to set the terms of the wager in such a way. We could have played a penny a point, or a pound for that matter. You were the one who chose to make it intimate.'

'True,' he agreed. 'But did you expect me to stand by and let you play with other men, under my very nose?'

'Frankly, I did not know what to expect,' she said, frowning for the first time. 'You have made it quite clear that you don't care for me in any real way and that I could seek pleasure where I liked. I did not think it would matter.'

The words stung, but he was unsure why. He had never planned on being a jealous fool when he married her. If he did not believe in fidelity, he could hardly expect it from her. But he hadn't thought she would grow restless so quickly. 'Until the matter of the heir is settled, I didn't expect you to show interest in other men,' he said.

'Oh,' she replied, and hesitated for a moment before saying, 'I was not there for the men, just the games.'

'Perhaps a ladies' card party would be more appropriate,' he suggested.

'Have you ever been to one?' she said, giving him a sceptical look. 'They are deadly dull. The stakes are low, and the talk is unceasing. I would much rather play with men who can keep their minds on the cards.'

He could not help it. He laughed. 'Perhaps you need different friends,' he said. 'I know several ladies who are almost as sharp as you with a deck of cards.'

'Then perhaps you should introduce me,' she said.

He thought of the Duchess of Belleville and the upcoming ball. What pernicious demon had caused him to accept that invitation? He forced himself to smile back at her. 'I shall, in time. But for now, perhaps you will claim your winnings.'

'In the carriage?' she said, surprised.

'I doubt there is anything we could do that would shock *my* driver,' he said.

She frowned. 'What I want is nothing so shocking. Simply a kiss.'

'You want me to kiss you,' he said, surprised. 'Just a kiss?'

'I had never been kissed before we married,' she said. 'And you have hardly kissed me since.'

'That is an exaggeration,' he said.

'Not on the lips,' she amended. 'Other places, certainly. But rarely on the mouth. And not for any length of time.'

That couldn't be true. He frowned, trying to remember all the things they had done together. 'What about at our wedding?' he said.

'The kind of kiss you can give in front of the vicar

is not the sort of kiss I expected from such a notorious man,' she said, giving him an encouraging smile.

He reached out and grabbed her hand, pulling her across the coach and into his arms. But that was too fast, wasn't it? What she was asking for should be slow and gentle, not rough and tumble. He relaxed his hold on her and watched her expression change from wide-eyed surprise to sleepy satisfaction. 'If I have a reputation to maintain, then I shall endeavour not to disappoint,' he said. He closed his eyes and put his lips to hers.

She was right. He had not kissed her like this before. He had ravaged her mouth as a prelude to ravaging her body. But he had forgotten how new she was to the art of love. There were things he took for granted that she had never done at all.

He brushed her lips again, taking the smallest taste of her, breathing in her breath, feeling the warmth of her skin close to his. How long had it been since he'd had a moment of such innocent sweetness with any woman? When he kissed her like this, he felt as virginal as she had been, as if the world was new and they were the only two people in it.

Or perhaps it was simply that he liked kissing her. He held her in his arms gently, as if she was something precious, and let his mouth explore hers, rubbing lip to lip and stroking his tongue against hers, not trying to inflame passion so much as learning the shape of her mouth, giving and taking a gentle pleasure that had been missing in the desperation of their bedroom encounters.

After a time, he pulled away, close enough so that his breath still brushed her cheek. 'Is that what you wanted?'

Her golden eyes shone beneath hooded lids and her lips were parted in a soft smile. 'It was very nice,' she whispered.

'I liked it as well,' he admitted. 'But then, there is much that I like about you.'

'Is there?' she said, leaning back to look at him.

She was fishing for compliments. In his extensive experience as a lover, it was not unusual for a woman to ask for reassurance after a moment of intimacy, and he always had the right words to keep them happy. At least until such a time as he was through with them.

But tonight, he stared back at her, his soul stripped bare and his mind awash with words he had used a hundred times before on women far less worthy of them. Then, before he could stop himself, he announced, 'You are an excellent card player.'

'Thank you,' she said. She disentangled her arms from his about his neck and slid out of his lap to take the seat at his side. 'Perhaps we shall play again sometime.'

'Perhaps,' he said, mortified by his own, graceless comment. Then he leaned back in his seat and stared ahead, waiting for the ride to end.

Chapter Eleven

When they arrived home, Julian escorted Portia to her room and sent her maid away. He peeled the clothes from her body and made love to her until they were both utterly spent.

But as they did so, she could not help wondering if he was thinking of her or someone else? Did it matter, so long as he was here with her?

Then, as he always did, he retired to his room and left her alone with her thoughts.

She shivered at the loss of him and pulled the covers up over her naked body, staring at the canopy above her. He had said that there was much to like about her. But when pressed on the subject, the best he could manage was that she had bested him at cards. It was hardly a declaration of undying love.

Was that even what she wanted from him? She wrapped her arms around herself, closed her eyes and thought of their kiss in the carriage until she fell asleep.

The next morning, he was gone from the house, as usual. She drifted through the day with no clear direction. She hesitated to call on old friends, for she did not want them to think that she was rushing to brag about her elevated status. But she had yet to receive visits from the wives of her husband's friends, since they had not yet appeared in public. And, after two visits to Bond Street in a week, she'd had enough shopping to last her for quite some time.

So, she remained in the house, finishing another of the books she had bought and watching the clock. She did not realise how tense she had grown while waiting until Julian returned, late in the afternoon, and she felt herself relax in the knowledge that he had come back to her.

She looked up at him with a smile as he passed the sitting room door. 'Good afternoon, Julian.'

He responded with a nod, but did not stop to speak to her. A moment later, she heard the door to his study close, a clear sign that he had no time for her. She did not fault him for it. It was not his job to entertain her. But she would have to find some way to keep busy or she would go mad with boredom.

Later, at dinner, she stared across the table at her husband, watching him eat. While she enjoyed the time they spent in bed, it was over all too soon, and when it was done, she felt no closer to him than she did now.

She was tempted to suggest that they go to the gaming hell again tonight, just to pass the time. But while it had been interesting once, she could not imagine doing it every night.

Now he stared back at her, setting down his fork and waiting for her to speak.

'Do you ever get bored?' she said, setting her fork to the side as well.

'No,' he said, staring back at her with a blank expression. 'There are many things to do in London, and I have ample means to enjoy them, whenever I want. You do as well,' he added. 'Your purse should be more than full after last night's winnings.'

'But you do the same things, day after day,' she said. 'At least, I assume you do. And see the same people while doing them.'

'Our friends,' he said firmly.

'Yours, perhaps,' she said with a faint smile. 'They are still strangers to me. The women of your set have made no overtures of friendship thus far.' She smiled to show him it did not bother her.

'The women of my set—' his brow furrowed as if he were seeking a diplomatic explanation '—are not in the habit of making morning calls here. It would not have been proper while I was unmarried. But I am sure, with time, you will be invited to their gatherings. The Duchess of Fallon has a mathematical salon that is quite popular.'

'I am not much for mathematics,' she admitted. 'But perhaps it would be interesting.' She took another bite of fish. 'I admire her dedication to an activity that she enjoys. It must give her great pleasure to fill her days thus.'

'I am sure it does,' he said, turning back to his meal.

A thought occurred to her. 'If I were to find some project,' she said with a vague wave of her hand. 'Something to occupy my time. Would you have any objection to my pursuing it?'

He stared at her for a moment, confused. 'You are not busy enough in your new role as duchess?'

'Truth be told, there is really not that much to do,' she admitted. 'Your servants are very well-trained and do not need much supervision.'

'There is shopping,' he suggested.

'Of course,' she agreed, trying not to wince.

'Parties. Balls. The events of the Season…'

'We have not gone to any, as of yet,' she reminded him. 'And even before we married, I'd had quite enough of the Season.'

'You were searching for a husband then,' he reminded her. 'Now that you are married, it will be different.'

'I suppose,' she agreed. 'But it's just that there is only so much of that one can do. And, with all the money you have, and all the power at your disposal, I wonder if there is a way to put it to good use.'

'You are dissatisfied with your life here?' he said, giving her an annoyed look.

'Not at all,' she said, hurriedly. 'I am more than content.'

'Except for the boredom,' he reminded her sharply.

'I did not mean to make it sound as if I am unhappy,' she said, wishing she had not spoken at all. 'I am just unaccustomed to having quite so much freedom.' She gave him what she hoped was an encouraging smile. 'I shall grow into my role in time, I am sure.'

'You are doing well, so far,' he said. 'More invitations arrived today. Answer some of them. We will go to whatever you wish.'

'There is a musicale next Wednesday,' she suggested.

'I am busy,' he replied before she could tell him more.

'Every Wednesday?' she asked.

He nodded. 'Make no plans for me then.'

'As you wish,' she said, biting her tongue to keep from asking why.

He smiled at her, sipping his wine. 'But tonight I am home with you.' Then he signalled for dessert.

That night, they made love, and the next day, he was gone again, and she was alone. But not as alone as she would be on Wednesday. It was still half a week away, but she could not seem to stop thinking about it. What appointment did he have that took place every week and was so vital it could not be changed? She pulled the bell to summon Banks.

When he arrived, she greeted him with a smile and asked, 'On Wednesdays, the Duke is in the habit of going out.'

'Yes, Your Grace,' he said, giving nothing more away.

'I assume he has left you no information as to what he does when he is away,' she said, searching his face for clues.

'No, Your Grace,' he said. 'He has the kitchen make up a basket and tells me to choose an appropriate wine to suit what they prepare. Then I summon the coach, and he is gone.'

She blinked in surprise. For a man who claimed to know nothing about the happenings in the house,

Banks's answer had been full of information. 'And did the Duke take the carriage today?'

'No, Your Grace. The equipage is available for your use, if you wish to go out.' This was followed by a direct stare, as if he was daring her to refuse the challenge.

'I think I should like that, Banks,' she replied. 'I am going up to change. Summon the coach for me.'

'Very good, Your Grace.'

She hurried upstairs and summoned her maid to help her change into a walking dress, struggling to contain her panic as Rose did up the buttons. None of the perfectly logical explanations she had assured herself she would find required a picnic basket and a bottle of wine.

She could think of only one reason to pack such a meal. It might be better to remain in ignorance than to learn such a truth. Why had Banks answered her question as he had? Wouldn't it have been kinder of him to tell a lie that would protect both master and mistress?

'A bonnet?' Rose said.

'With a veil, please,' Portia replied. It would not be as effective as a mask, but it would give her some anonymity. Once the hat was in place, she went down the stairs and out to the street, marching up to the front of the carriage and gesturing that the coachman come down to speak with her.

He followed her instructions warily, as if he guessed that he would not want to fulfil the order she was about to give.

'Where does he go on Wednesdays?' she asked, not bothering with details.

The man gave her a worried look, and said, 'I do not think it is wise for you to go there.'

Neither did she, come to that. But she had come this far, and it would be an act of cowardice to turn back now. 'Take me to the place he goes,' she said. When the man still hesitated, she said, 'I order you to do so.'

'All right, Your Grace,' he said with a sigh and helped her up into the carriage. They drove for several minutes through Westminster until they were in St John's Wood. Then the carriage stopped in front of a charming little villa with a blue door. The coachman made no effort to open the door for her. Apparently, her previous instruction had been fulfilled.

Portia stared at the house for a moment, unsure of what she should do next. When they'd set out, she'd still had hopes that she might be wrong. Perhaps the destination would turn out to be an opium den or a brothel. But even a discreet source of corruption should have some indication that it was a public venue.

This was clearly a residential neighbourhood, and they had stopped at someone's home.

She should not have come here. She did not want to know anything more, nor had she wished to call attention to her presence by sitting outside the house of her husband's mistress in a carriage emblazoned with his family crest.

Now it was too late. As she stared at it, the front door opened and a dark-haired woman stood in the entry, staring at the carriage and smiling in welcome. She was hoping for a surprise visit from Julian. Judging by the warmth of her smile, she knew him. She loved him.

Portia felt a rush of panic and tapped on the wall of the carriage, opening the little door to speak to the coachman. 'Drive,' she said, closing her eyes as if it was possible to shut out the truth.

Without a word of response from the driver, the coach was rolling away, down the street, around a corner and back into traffic towards the townhouse.

The coachman had been right. This, of all things, was something she was not prepared to see. If her husband had a mistress, it would have been better not to know of it. Especially not one as beautiful and unassuming as that one had been.

It might have been easier if the girl had looked the part of a kept woman. If she'd been wearing jewels in the daytime and too much rouge, if she'd been older and coarser and blowsy. But she had looked like the sort of woman that Portia could be friends with, who would share her confidences.

And the thought that, just days after their wedding, he had gone to her and…

She stuffed her hand in her mouth to stop the sob and sank back into the plush red upholstery of the carriage seat, wishing that she could disappear into it and never have to face the pitying look that the driver would give her, when they arrived back at the townhouse.

Once there, she made sure that her veil was in place as he helped her out of the carriage and went from the front door directly to her room. She did not come out again until she was sure that she had full control of her emotions. She refused to cry over something that could not be helped.

Her mother had warned her, but she had been sure that she could keep her heart safe and untouched. It had been only a few days, and she cared more about her husband's behaviour than she'd thought it possible to care about anything.

It was because she'd convinced herself that he could limit himself to one woman, if only for a while. She took another deep breath and closed her eyes, exhaling slowly and telling herself that she could let go of the pain as easily.

She must remember that she was not his lover, she was his wife. She would be the mother of his children. It was more than the other woman had, surely. He was hers on Wednesday afternoons, but that was not so very much time when one added up the hours in a lifetime.

If he could be Portia's at other times? If she could carve out random bits of his days and nights with lovemaking and talk of poetry and perhaps even a few card games. That would be enough.

Perhaps, if she told herself this often enough, it would become the truth.

That night, when Julian came home to dinner, something had changed. The look that Banks gave him as he came through the main door was one of profound disappointment, even though he was arriving home sober and in daylight with the intention of staying the evening.

Julian smiled back at him, refusing to be cowed. But when he went upstairs to his room, his valet stared at him with similar reproach.

'Is everything all right, Mason?' he asked, as the servant dressed him for dinner.

'Of course, Your Grace,' Mason replied, and tugged

the knot a fraction of an inch tighter than it needed to be.

Julian slipped a finger between linen and neck and tugged until it was comfortable. Then he shrugged into his coat and went down to dinner.

Once there, he found a bone in his fish.

He removed it with a deft flick of his knife and glanced over at his wife. As always, she was elegant, gracious and everything he could have hoped for.

And wrong.

Perhaps it was the quiet that bothered him. She was not trying to engage him in conversation, as she usually did. She did not even comment on the quality of the meal, which was exceptional tonight, except for the fishbone.

'How was your day,' he asked at last, just to break the tension in the room.

'Fine,' she said favouring him with a smile that was far too bright.

'What did you do?' he asked, remembering her complaint of boredom the previous day.

'Nothing of interest,' she replied, and went back to her meal.

After dinner, they retired to the sitting room, and she picked at her needlework while he read aloud from one of her novels, hoping that this would change the mood.

She was grateful, of course. The very picture of the wife he imagined he would have when he married. And later, when he took her to bed, she was as willing as ever.

Too willing, if that was possible. Her touch was too eager. Her eyes shone with a light he did not recognise, as if she was not seeing him at all, but something else entirely.

He stopped his kisses and held her away from him, staring into her face, searching for an answer. 'What is wrong?' he asked.

In response, her smile grew even brighter than before. It dazzled him, and he felt desire rising in him again, a primal emotion oblivious to truth or lies, blindly wanting the pleasure that came from being with her.

'Nothing,' she said, shaking her head and looking past him, baring her throat for another kiss.

He resisted. 'No. There is something.'

She pulled away, staring at him, and shook her head. But her next smile was late, as if she'd had to manufacture it before it reached her lips. 'I am fine,' she said firmly. Then she lay down on the bed, waiting for him to mount her.

He stared at her, baffled. When they had married, he'd assumed he'd soon grow tired of her and his life would go back to normal. He'd never imagined that she would be the one to take a distaste to him. But it seemed this was so.

'We do not have to do anything tonight, if you are in no mood…'

'That is all right,' she insisted, staring up at him and shifting slightly to make room for him on the bed.

His desire did not exactly wither, though it was certainly not what it had been when they'd retired. But he was unwilling to go back to his room without trying to turn the tide.

He closed his eyes and leaned forward over her, inhaling her scent. It made him feel happy and sad at the same time, just to be in the same room with her. It was his home. There was no reason he should not feel at ease here. But he never had. If he stayed too long here, he was usually overcome with the desire to be elsewhere.

Yet now, just when he was pretty sure he was not welcome in her bed, he could not seem to bring himself to go back to his own. And to go out and seek pleasure elsewhere would be even worse.

So he lay down beside her, close enough so they were touching from shoulder to toes, and wrapped an arm around her, pulling her even closer to him.

She gave an exasperated sigh, softening slightly but still holding her true self apart from him, even though they could not have been closer.

'I think, tonight, this will be enough,' he said, kissing her bare shoulder. 'Just to be with you. I want…' What did he want? Anything she would allow him. 'To stay here,' he finished, surprising himself. 'For a while, at least,' he amended.

'All right,' she said quietly, and somehow the barrier she'd placed between them slipped and things were as they had been. He forced himself to relax, afraid that any move he made would upset this new, delicate balance. Instead, he closed his eyes and tried to sleep.

Portia lay still beside him, eyes open and baffled by the way the evening had gone. At first she had planned to confront him, to demand to know who the woman was and what his intentions were towards her in the future.

But she was afraid that the answer would be exactly what she thought it was. That would be followed by the blunt reminder that it was none of her business.

But now, here he was at her side, offering her the warmth of his body and the simple joy of being near him with no obligation to do more.

She sighed and he stirred against her, his hold on her tightening slightly before he settled again.

She rolled onto her side to look at him and was surprised to see his eyes were open as well.

'I do not want to keep you awake,' he said easing away and giving her an absent-minded kiss on the lips.

'I would not mind,' she said, her arm snaking around his neck to pull him back to her. 'You never stay with me, after.'

'Is that so important?' he asked.

'It might be,' she said, then admitted the truth. 'I like having you with me.'

'And I like to watch you sleep,' he said, kissing her again. His lips were on her skin again, not so much arousing as soothing.

'And you?'

'I do not sleep,' he said with a wan smile. 'At least, not well.'

She leaned on an elbow to look at him. 'How long has this been going on?'

'For years,' he admitted.

'Perhaps, a doctor...'

He shook his head. 'They would only give me laudanum, and I assure you, that is no healthier than the methods I have chosen to deal with my wakefulness.'

'The places you go, the things you do...'

'Which you promised not to question,' he reminded her. But he did not seem annoyed by her enquiry. 'I am able to get some rest when I am tired enough. Usually a few hours in the morning, a nap at the club in the afternoon...' He shrugged. 'But in the evenings,

I am restless. I do not go out every night,' he added. 'Some nights I stay at home and read.'

'Which explains your love of poetry,' she said with a smile.

He nodded. 'It passes the nighttime hours.'

She drummed her fingers on his shoulder before reaching up to caress his temples. 'Perhaps I shall learn to stay awake with you, to keep you company.'

'Then two of us would be unhappy and afflicted,' he said wryly. 'I would not wish that on you.'

'But at least you would not be lonely,' she said.

'Lonely.' He frowned as if he'd never heard the word.

'You must be,' she replied. 'When I found you at the gaming hell, no friends were with you. You do not speak of companions. No one visits you here.' She thought of the house in St John's Wood and the woman there, wondering if she was his only companion.

'It is not as bad as all that,' he said quickly. 'I was on excellent terms with Westbridge until recently.'

'How awkward,' she said with a frown.

'And I have you,' he reminded her.

'But you rarely speak if I do not prompt you to,' she said.

'Perhaps I have nothing in me worth saying,' he said.

'I would like to hear you, all the same,' she said.

'If we are to make a life together,' she whispered, 'I wish to know you for who you really are.'

'I am sorry that I cannot be more for you,' he said with a sad smile. 'You must learn to accept that there is nothing more to see.' After a final kiss that was as slow and soft as the one he'd given her in the carriage, he rose from the bed and went to his room.

A short time later, she heard his footsteps on the main stairs and the sound of the front door closing as he left the house.

Chapter Twelve

What had possessed him to come here?

Julian glanced around the receiving room of Miss Faukland's Temple of Love and wondered, as he always did, if the eponymous Miss F existed, or if it was a *nom de guerre* for some ageing madam who had found there was better money in keeping a stable than in working alone.

Whoever she was, she kept a fine establishment, where the loveliest ladies catered to the most discriminating gentlemen. The champagne they were plying him with was as fine as anything in his own cellar, and the posture moll standing naked on a table at the centre of the room was both lovely and shockingly flexible.

But could he consider himself an epicurean if he had left the bed of a beautiful and desirable woman to settle for a whore?

At least the whores never asked him difficult questions. He had been ready to sleep beside Portia, or at least pretend to, lying innocently next to her and making no demands. Then she had begun to quiz him on the contents of his mind.

He drained his glass, wishing that it was something strong enough to take away the sting of her questions. She claimed that she wanted to know him, as if she had not seen everything there was to see. He was a gambler, a wastrel, a seducer of women. She might think he had married her to make up for that damned duel, but his true motives had been lust and a desire to see her punished for her mercenary nature.

She had no right to touch him so tenderly and act as if she had ever wanted anything from him but his money. It was far better to be here, lying with a woman who did not pretend to care than lying to himself at home. How addled had he become that he had convinced himself that he would rest easy on such weak gruel as chaste kisses and sweet words?

He would have some more champagne and then perhaps a redhead. Or a brunette. Anything but a hazel-eyed blonde. He signalled for more wine and a dainty hand reached out to steady his as its owner filled his glass.

He glanced up at the girl who was serving him and she smiled, sliding onto the divan beside him and taking a sip from the glass he held, staining the rim with the rouge from her lips. She was a ginger beauty, already stripped to her stays and shift. She smelled of perfume and musk. Her gaze was coquettish, her smile so practiced that he could almost believe it was sincere.

Though she was sitting so close to him that he could feel her body's heat through the wool of his coat, he shivered. A week ago, what happened next would have been a certainty. They'd have taken the champagne bottle and adjourned to one of the anonymous bedrooms upstairs. He'd have been done with her in less than a half an hour. Or perhaps he'd have requested that she summon a friend to add some spice to their encounter.

He shivered again.

'Are you ill?' Her smile did not falter, but suspicion glittered in her eyes.

'Yes,' he lied, and felt her easing away from him, possibly fearing a contagion.

'I should probably go home,' he said. 'To my own bed.'

'Another time, perhaps,' she said, still smiling.

'Perhaps,' he said. It was another lie. But then, everything here was a lie. He had simply never noticed it before.

Portia waited only a few moments after Julian had left her before lighting a candle and searching for her slippers. She slipped a wrapper over her nightgown and crept down the stairs to where Banks was snuffing candles and barring the door for the night.

'Where has he gone?' she said, giving the butler a look that warned him she was in no mood for his usual obfuscation.

'It would be unwise to follow him, Your Grace,' Banks replied, returning her gaze without flinching.

'I am aware of that,' she said.

'He summoned the carriage,' Banks added. 'He will likely send it back when he arrives at his destination, for he prefers to walk home.'

Compared to their usual interactions, Banks was proving to be a wealth of information. 'Summon me when the coach returns. I am going out.'

'Very good, Your Grace.'

She went back up the stairs to her room, closing the door behind her and staring into the mirror at her own reflection.

You are not what he wants.

The words echoed in her head, a bitter commentary on the success of her marriage. First, it had been the mysterious woman in St John's Wood. And tonight?

Banks had not needed to tell her the whole truth. Her husband had left her bed to seek out a whore. He had said that he'd wanted nothing more than to lie next to her and pretend to sleep. But in truth, he'd wanted more, and she was not sure what that was.

Her hair was braided. Perhaps that was the problem. He liked it loose. And although she had been willing when he'd come to her, had she been too passive?

Her heart had not been fully his tonight. She was angry after the trip to St John's Wood. He had probably sensed it. But if he was willing to settle for some anonymous light-skirts, he should not have minded her lack of sincere affection.

She glared at the woman in the mirror: a naive girl who had been so sure she could be a worthy wife but could not hold her husband's attention for even a week. She was not a duchess. She was a failure. A nothing. There was a battle going on in this house, and the girl in the mirror was a victim, not a warrior.

Things had to change.

She stripped off the wrapper and pulled the nightgown over her head, balling it up and tossing it to the floor. Then she stared at her naked body, considering.

She was no authority on the female form, but she saw no obvious deficiencies in hers. She ran a hand lightly across her breasts, watching as the skin flushed and the nipples tightened. Julian had praised her responsiveness when they were together and called her beautiful. This body was not the problem.

She tugged the ribbon from her hair, untwining

the braid and running her fingers through the locks, shaking her head until the waves were a wild mane. She bit her lip and pinched her cheeks until the colour blazed in her face. She looked wild, dangerous and still a little angry.

What had Julian said on the first night, about the emotion of the moment overcoming all others? Perhaps that was what he wanted. An experience that transcended thought.

Tonight, she was angry.

No. She had been angry. Now she was furious. If Julian wanted oblivion, she would be happy to send him there. She just had to find him first.

There was a soft knock on the door, and Banks announced from the other side that the carriage was waiting at the front of the house.

'I will be down in a moment,' she said. She grabbed a cloak from the wardrobe, swathing herself from head to foot and pulling the hood over her messy hair. Then, she went down the stairs and out of the house to where the coachman waited and ordered him back to the place he had just left.

Julian walked out of the brothel and into the street, inhaling the scents of the night: urine, vomit, coal smoke and the ever-present odour of horse. The air outside the house was as foul as the activities were within. He needed to get away from it. He did not know his destination, but tonight, walking might not be enough. Perhaps he needed to run, if only to get rid of the excess energy jittering along his nerves.

Then, down the street, he spotted his carriage, which should be in the mews behind the house and not waiting here for him. He paced down the street towards it and glared at the driver.

'Home, Your Grace?' the man said quickly before he could get a word out.

'Damn it, yes,' Julian said, throwing his arms up in frustrated surrender. 'Home.' Perhaps he would go back to Portia's bed, though he was hardly in the mood. He did not wait for the coachman's help but yanked open the door and kicked down the step, climbing in and shutting the door before throwing himself into his seat and glaring into the darkness.

He was not alone.

The silent woman on the seat across from him was heavily cloaked and largely in shadow. She must have wandered into the wrong carriage. Though his eyes were still adjusting to the darkness, he suspected she could see him well enough to realise that he was not whoever she'd been waiting for. In a moment she would offer a drunken giggle and a slurred apology. And then she would be gone.

But, as the carriage started to move, she threw back her hood.

'Portia.' The name came out of him in a choked whisper. For, though it was definitely his wife, this was not the woman he'd left an hour ago.

She undid the tie of her cloak and pushed it away, shocking him further. Under it, she was wearing nothing but her slippers. As he watched, she kicked those away as well and raised one leg, resting her foot on the carriage seat and spreading her thighs wide, displaying her charms as brazenly as the girl that had been posing in the brothel.

She raised her hand to cup her breast and stared at him, squeezed it and bit her lip with a sigh.

He forced his breath to remain steady, counting to three with each inhale, each exhale.

Her hand slipped between her legs. She was playing with herself. No. She was playing with him. Her fingers spread her sex and stroked. Her back arched and she shuddered. Once. Twice. Three times.

Her eyes had been closed and she opened them to stare at him. Then she dropped her foot to the floor and stood. With feline grace, she moved across the carriage to straddle him.

Their lips met. The kiss she gave him was nothing like the one they had shared here after visiting the gaming hell. This kiss was as hard as he was, full of teeth. It bruised, as if she wished to punish him for daring to leave her.

He wanted it. He deserved it.

She pulled away and reached up to tug at his cravat, which was still uncomfortably tight, smiling as he gasped before she slowly undid the knot. She sat back and admired her work.

Did she really mean to make love to him in a carriage? She had been the aggressor, but now he was not sure if she was waiting for him to take the lead. It would serve him right if she had excited him only to deny him.

He reached between them and fumbled with the flap of his breeches, trying to expose himself to her.

She pushed his hands away and smiled. And still, she did not move.

Did she need more time? Was she not already aroused? He was more than ready, painfully hard. It would kill him if she waited much longer. Did she want him to pray? To beg? He would do so. He was hers.

As if she sensed his thoughts, her hands drifted down to his lap. She took her time, lingering over each fastening until he was dizzy with anticipation. At last, he was free and she was lowering her body onto him, moving on him in time with the rocking of the carriage.

'Is this what you wanted tonight?' she whispered,

planting a hand on either side of his head so she could use the wall of the carriage to balance.

'God.' He couldn't think. Her thighs were squeezing his, the muscles inside her clenching like a hand.

She leaned forward to kiss him, biting his lip. 'Can the women in that place do this to you?' she said, rising up on her knees and offering him a breast.

He took it, sucking the nipple into his mouth, only to have her pull it away again.

He whimpered. Dear God, she had unmanned him. But then she offered her breasts again, and he buried his face in them, leaning forward as she lowered herself once more and began to move again.

'Tell me you are mine,' she said, her hips tightening.

'Yours,' he murmured, barely able to think, much less speak. She had taken him to the brink and was holding him there.

She relaxed and the pressure eased, the pleasure dimmed. 'Swear it.'

'I am yours,' he said, desperate again. 'I swear on all that is holy. Just… Just…'

She moved again in that special way she had found, finishing him with a grind of her hips, leaving him weak and sated.

Then, without a word, she eased off him and returned to her seat, slipping into her shoes and wrapping up in the cloak again.

The carriage came to a stop and he rushed to do up his breeches as the coachman came to open the door and help them out.

She exited before he did, her movements smooth and graceful beneath the cape, giving no hint of the secrets hidden beneath it. Her manner was so ordinary that he could almost believe what had happened between them was a dream.

But it had been almost too real. If he did not believe it for himself, he had only to look at Banks, who greeted them at the door. The butler's face was as impassive as always, but there was a twinkle in his eye and the slightest inclination of his head as he greeted the two of them, as if he might allow himself to grin once they were both properly out of sight.

Unable to help himself, Julian grinned back at him and turned to his wife as she walked past him and up the stairs, as impassive as a queen before her subjects. She disappeared into her room without bothering to wish him goodnight.

Julian stared after her for a moment, still dazed. Then he went to his own bed and, for the first time in a long time, slept well.

When Portia woke, it was nearly eleven. She stretched and smiled, then rang for Rose. She washed and dressed in her most flattering day gown, a yellow muslin as bright and sunny as her mood.

Last night had been more than just exciting. It had been a triumph. She had shown Julian who she could be and what she could do. And he had sworn himself to her in a way that was more real, more sincere than any of the empty vows he had made in front of the vicar. They belonged together. They belonged to each other. She was happier than she'd imagined possible.

She went down to see about breakfast.

On her way to the dining room, she passed Banks in the hall. 'Has His Grace come down yet?' she asked, giving him a smile that she hoped might finally break through his reserve.

The butler nodded, as distant as ever. 'He has gone already, Your Grace.' His mouth twitched as if the next words pained him. 'It is Wednesday, after all.'

Chapter Thirteen

She ate her breakfast, her smile frozen on her face as the joy behind it evaporated. She had been a fool to think that last night had changed anything. It had taught her one thing, she supposed. There was pleasure in taking the initiative when making love, a certain thrill in having the upper hand. But though he had seemed to enjoy it, and she had forced a declaration from him, it had meant nothing. Julian's plans for the day had not changed.

She must remember that she had made plans as well. She had intended to keep her mind and body too busy to care about his absence. Last night had been nothing more than a distraction for both of them. She had wanted it to be more, but she must remember that wanting did not make a thing so. She had a perfectly good marriage. It was not a love match, but she had never believed in such things and was not about to start now.

She walked to Bond Street for a final fitting on the gown for tomorrow night's ball. The finished dress was splendid. It was some consolation that, when she made her first appearance as the Duchess of Septon, she would be the talk of the *ton*. When the fitting was through, she rewarded herself with a trip to Gunter's and another to Hatchards, telling herself that a good book was all the company she needed for the rest of the day.

When he returned home after supper, she smiled and pretended that nothing was wrong, welcoming her husband into her bed and making love with him, even while imagining another woman's perfume on his skin and seeing other hands touching him each time she closed her eyes. She lay awake as he returned to his own room, willing herself to think of nothing at all.

The next evening, they were to go to the Duchess of Belleville's ball, and Portia welcomed this as a much-needed distraction from her husband's probable infidelity. As usual, he was absent from the house in the morning but returned in midafternoon and went to his study to work.

It was some consolation that she would not have to hunt him down when the moment came to go, but she could not help a feeling of dread at what the night might bring. Before they'd married, she'd gone largely unnoticed by the *ton*, her come out inauspicious and her courtships equally so. Now she would be on the arm of one of the most notorious men in London. The thought of so many eyes turned in her direction made her stomach flutter like it was full of moths.

She went to her room to find that her gown had arrived from the modiste's. It lay spread on her bed, a sea of mossy green satin shining against the white of the counterpane. Lying in the middle of the skirt was an open jewel box that held a parure of the topaz Julian had promised. He must have spirited it upstairs when he'd returned home, leaving it for her as a surprise.

She sat down on the bed and stared in amazement at the delicate gold necklace and the eardrops and hairpins that matched it. When he had talked of jewels, she had imagined something heavy and pretentious that would scream her rank to the others in the room. But this was so light and finely wrought that it would lie like a whisper on her skin and frame her face with light.

It would have been better, she supposed, if he had come to give it to her in person. Perhaps, when the time came to dress, she would ask him for help with the clasp. Or would that seem too needy? Maybe a simple thank you was all he was expecting. She was his wife and not his lover. It would be better to maintain her dignity now, so she did not lose it when next Wednesday came.

When it was time to dress, she allowed Rose to help her into the gown and dress her hair with the gold clips included with the necklace. When they were finished, she hardly recognised her reflection in the dressing table mirror. She looked like a woman, not a girl, more elegant, more beautiful than she ever had before. A proper duchess, she hoped, who could hold her head high through the gossip that was sure to be swirling around her tonight.

As she came down the stairs, Julian was at the foot looking up at her, and for a moment his expression changed. Was it surprise? Amazement? Or something more like hunger? She could not tell. But it gave her the confidence to continue serenely down the stairs to him and accept his outstretched hand.

'My dear,' he said, the faintest softness in his voice.

'Julian,' she replied, forcing her fears to the back of her mind.

'You are magnificent,' he said in that same awed tone. 'As I knew you would be.'

Her reserve faltered and she felt herself blush at the compliment.

'Let us go,' he said. 'Though, at the sight of you, I'd much rather remain at home.' Then he raised her hand to kiss her knuckles before returning it to the crook of his arm and leading her to the carriage. As they took their places across from each other, his expression sobered. 'There is something I must tell you before we arrive,' he said, shifting in his seat.

'What might that be?' she said, hoping that it might be another compliment.

'The hostess of tonight's event…' he began cautiously.

'The Duchess of Belleville,' she supplied. To prepare for the evening, she had read the guide to the peerage from cover to cover, memorising such details as might help her with the people she might meet.

'We have a history,' he said. Then he gave her a significant look, waiting for her response.

It took a moment for her to understand that he was referring to something that would never appear in Debrett's. 'You are lovers,' she said, stunned.

'Were,' he corrected. 'What happened between us has been over for some time, and I have no intention of revisiting it.'

'And you are telling me this only now,' she said, staring out the window to find that they were nearly at their destination.

'I did not want you worrying about it before you needed to,' he said. 'You will meet other such women, when we go about together.'

'Will I?' she said, her good mood disappearing. 'And who knows of this affair?'

'Most people, I should think,' he said, shifting again. 'Such liaisons are common between people of our class, once the wives have provided their husbands with male children.'

'You have alluded to that before,' she said. 'But you did not tell me what you had done.'

'This was an open secret amongst the *ton*,' he said with a dismissive shake of his head.

'To everyone but me,' she snapped. She had been far too insignificant to share in such gossip.

'That is why I am telling you, now,' he said patiently, as if this explained it all. 'You knew of my reputation when you came to me.'

'I did,' she agreed. But she had not imagined that it might affect her so directly. She raised her hand to the necklace at her throat, wondering if it was some sort of bribe to keep her loyalty through what was likely to be a difficult evening.

'Do not worry,' he said, as if she could do anything but. 'There will be no embarrassing scenes, if you do not choose to make them.'

'Of course, not,' she said. 'You are all far too civilised for that. And I?' She shrugged and smiled at him. 'What you do does not matter a jot to me.'

To her surprise, he flinched. But he recovered almost immediately, giving her his usual, seductive smile. 'Of course not,' he echoed, then glanced out the window. 'I think we have arrived. Let me help you down.'

He led her from the carriage to the ballroom, and she did her best not to gape at her surroundings, which were more sumptuous than any she had seen before. The Septon townhouse did not have a ballroom, but she suspected the manor did. In time, she would be hosting gatherings as opulent as this one, with the same august guest list. She must not lose her nerve in the face of her own future.

She gave the man beside her a sidelong glance, and he returned one of his own, instantly aware of her attention. 'It will be fine,' he said to no one in particular.

'Of course,' she said, lifting her chin an inch as they entered the ballroom. As they were announced, their hostess rushed forward, taking her husband by the hands. 'Jooo-lian!' She crooned the name, beaming at him as if his presence was the thing she had been awaiting all evening.

He smiled back at her, disentangling himself from her embrace. 'Honoria. So good to see you again. May I present my wife, Portia.'

The Duchess's smile dimmed as she turned to Portia, and her eyes glittered, bright and hard as diamonds. 'Ah, yes. Your sudden marriage to the girl you duelled with Westbridge over.'

Julian gave a cavalier shrug and a brilliant smile. Then he reached out to clasp Portia's hand.

Since he was offering no explanation, she spoke for him. 'It is not often that a man makes such a dramatic statement of his affection. I could hardly refuse him after that.' She waited anxiously, fearing that he would laugh and explain that the situation was quite the opposite of what she described, but he said nothing, instead turning his smile on her.

After a gaze that lasted a moment longer than needed, he turned back to the Duchess. 'We are delighted to be here. So glad you invited us. And now, we will leave you to your other guests.' With a gentle tug on her hand, he pulled her towards the dance floor.

When they were out of earshot of their hostess, Portia let out a sigh of relief. Then she turned back to him with a frozen smile. 'That was delightful. Just how many of your ex-lovers am I likely to meet tonight?'

He glanced around the room, and she was annoyed to realise that he was counting. 'Three,' he muttered.

'Including the Duchess?'

'Four,' he amended.

This was what she got for ignoring her mother's warning. Now she had stumbled blindly into a nest of vipers, sure that she could handle herself. She must prove that she had the poise needed to be up to the task.

'Do you have anything you wish to say,' Julian said, glancing in her direction.

'No,' she replied, staring at the crowd around them.

'Then let me introduce you to some of the other guests.' He led her about the room, stopping at one group, then another and another, presenting her to peers and their ladies, with a smile so bright she was unable to stop herself from beaming back at him.

Could it really be true that all these people knew of his affair with the hostess? No one seemed shocked by his presence here or his sudden marriage to her.

If anything, they were delighted. Though he had claimed to have no intimates, men greeted him as if they were close friends and offered him warm congratulations on their union. Their wives blushed and laughed as he flirted with them, charmed by his comments. They smiled at her as if she was the luckiest woman in the room.

Indeed, she felt like it. He interspersed his teasing banter with others with glances at her that were so full of affection that she could almost believe in the love match they pretended to be.

Had he lain with any of the women they'd spoken with so far? It was not as if she didn't care. But after listening to him charm the room and watching him turn that charm back on her, she wanted to believe that behaviour was a thing of the past. She wanted to forgive his sins and be with the man he could be, when he wanted to.

Now they had reached the back of the room, where there was a door that led to a small salon where cards were being played. He turned to her and raised both of her hands to kiss them. 'There,' he said, as if a duty had been dispensed with. 'Now that you are not amongst strangers, I will leave you to the dancing.'

'You are leaving me?' she said, trying not to look as panicked as she felt.

'Not for long,' he assured her. 'I will be in the card room with the other married gentlemen. Please, save the waltz for me.'

'Of course,' she replied, forcing herself to smile as he left her alone. She should have expected this. It was not as if other husbands and wives hung on each other when out in public. It would be rude of them to behave as if they were courting and could not get enough of each other's company. The looks he'd just given her were nothing more than charm, which was really nothing like sincerity at all.

But they were so recently married, she'd thought some attention was warranted. Then she remembered that, though he was very attentive in bed, he had shared that particular form of attention with several other women here tonight, and he was not spending time with them either.

'Lady Septon,' her hostess called, hurrying across the room towards her with the smile of a wolf greeting a lamb. 'I must introduce you to some of my other guests. They are dying to meet you. I doubt you would have made their acquaintance before your recent marriage.'

This was a dig, she supposed, at the fact that her parents were of no real pedigree. Though they might have met a baron or two, her mother stood in awe of even the lowliest rank. But now a duchess was eager to make introductions for her. She could guess the reason why.

She returned the predatory grin with a polite smile. 'My husband has made the introductions already. He is very solicitous.'

'Not to these friends, I am sure,' the Duchess said, and stepped out of the way to reveal three equally ferocious-looking females, who were staring at her in curiosity.

'May I present, the Duchess of Ashcroft, the Countess of Fairhaven and Viscountess Montrose.'

The ladies gathered round her, and as they exchanged greetings, Portia struggled to resist the feeling that she was caught in a wave and being carried out to sea. As if she was actually swimming, she took a deep breath and let it out slowly to bolster her smile. She must remember that she was on equal footing with these ladies and not some interloper.

Then Viscountess Montrose said the words that Portia most feared to hear. 'We are all old friends of your husband.'

'Very good friends,' the Duchess of Ashcroft added spitefully.

She meant lovers, Portia supposed. Jealousy had moved them to gather against her, just to make the evening difficult. This would be the tenor of all future interactions, if she did not take control of the situation immediately.

She smiled back at them, her mind racing. 'How nice for you,' she said, keeping her tone neutral.

'Very nice,' the Countess of Fairhaven said, smirking. 'But then, you would know what a good friend he can be.'

Portia's stomach knotted. It had been foolish of her to imagine that he felt anything more or different for her than he had for his other lovers. He was a practiced seducer, and she just his latest conquest.

She forced her smile to be even brighter and signalled a passing footman for a glass of champagne. She rolled the stem of her wine glass between her fingers as she searched for a witty retort. 'As his wife, of course I do,' she said, grabbing for the only advantage she had over these harpies.

'His wife,' Honoria repeated, unable to keep the jealousy from her voice. 'We are all wondering how you managed to capture him. He has been a most elusive target for years.'

Portia glanced around the circle and gathered her nerve. 'Well, it helps if one is unmarried to begin with.'

As one, the ladies around her sucked breath through their teeth and she knew that the barb had struck home. She pushed on. 'And, of course, there was the matter of the duel.'

'It was a terrible scandal,' Honoria reminded her.

If she must be infamous, she would learn to enjoy it as these women did their adulteries. 'Over me,' she agreed with a dazed smile. 'It is quite hard to resist a man who is so moved to come to my defence that he is willing to risk his life.'

She glanced around the circle and said, 'But not everyone is so lucky as to have such a devoted spouse, I suppose.'

Mouths widened in shock at this, and the Countess forced a laugh. 'Ahh, the folly of young love.'

The other women nodded. 'In time, you will learn that it is one thing to capture a rake and quite another to keep him,' the Duchess of Ashcroft replied.

'Julian is easily bored,' Honoria agreed. 'And on to the next diversion in no time.'

'You would know that better than I, being such an old friend,' Portia said, giving the slightest emphasis to the word *old*.

'And you are a child,' the woman snapped back, before regaining control again. 'If he is so devoted, where is he now?'

She forced herself to keep her gaze on the challenger and not search the room for rescue. 'I do not plan to keep him in my pocket, if that is what you expect. It matters not where he is each moment of the evening, so long as I know we are going home together at the end of it.'

But did she know that? What would she do if he made some excuse and put her in the carriage alone?

She would worry about that when the time came. For the moment, she could enjoy the shocked look on her hostess's face. 'You think that, just because he married you, he will be loyal?'

'I think, no matter what he does, I will still be his wife,' she said pointedly, refusing to look away.

'And did he give you that necklace?' the Countess asked curiously.

'A wedding gift,' Portia replied, her hand going to her throat.

'Not one of his mother's,' Honoria said, squinting

at the stones. 'She had exquisite taste in jewellery, as I remember. A beautiful collection, in addition to the estate jewellery.'

So, the topaz parure was new, just as her wedding ring had been. What did that mean? The Duchess seemed to think it was lesser. Should she be hurt?

She would decide later. For now, she refused to show it. 'I did not know you were old enough to remember his mother,' she said, returning veiled insult with veiled insult.

'Everyone knew of her,' the other duchess said dismissively. 'Everyone that mattered, at least.' She gave Portia a smile to remind her that her ignorance put her firmly out of that category.

She smiled back and said, 'I am sure my husband will tell me all I wish to know when we return to the manor and he gives me the jewels in the lock room. But he was quite adamant that I have something to wear immediately. He is too kind.' She ran a finger along her new necklace to show she was not bothered.

'Too kind indeed,' Honoria agreed.

'Just as you are,' Portia said. 'I have taken far too much of your time, this evening. Surely, your other guests…'

'Do not be silly,' Honoria said, taking her arm in a vice-like grip. 'I would not dream of leaving you friendless. Nor would the other ladies, I am sure. We shall be with you all evening.'

'All evening,' Portia repeated with a frozen smile. 'And it is early, yet.'

'Indeed,' said Honoria, and signalled a servant for more champagne.

Julian walked into the card room, accepting a drink as he took his seat, his mind on the woman he'd left behind. He'd intended to hurt her when he'd told her to accept this invitation, to wave his previous affair with Honoria in her face. She was the one who had wanted this marriage. She should have to pay the price for it.

It had been petty of him. He should not have waited until tonight to tell her the truth. It was clear from their brief interaction that Honoria meant to cause trouble, and he had abandoned Portia to it, proving himself a coward all over again.

As the man across the table from him dealt, he tried to focus on the cards in his hand. But his mind was drawn back to the woman in the other room and the men who remained there with her. How many of them were husbands of his former lovers, who might be trying to lay the groundwork for a flirtation?

He'd told himself for years that his behaviour was far from unusual. After successions were secured, more couples agreed to separate lives and pleasures and did not dig too deeply into the comings and goings of their spouses. It would likely be the same with him and Portia. He knew for certain that he did not plan to remain faithful.

At least that had not been his intent when he'd married her. But now something about the *ton's* cavalier attitude towards marriage rankled.

And there had been that abortive trip to the brothel. And the way it had ended…

That was but one night, he reminded himself. He only had to look to his own parents to see that the image of lifelong fidelity was a pretty façade over a decayed foundation.

But he was not like his father, was he? He had never bothered with false fronts, preferring to wear his wickedness out where all could see. And though Portia might share his mother's mercenary nature, she had done very little to provoke him, thus far. There was an unexpected sweetness to her, a gentleness that he had not seen in his mother or in any of his previous lovers. A fire, as well.

She might grow hard and cold with time, of course.

But if she did, he would be the cause of it. He had abandoned her to Honoria and her friends, and so he could not be surprised if she grew calluses on her tender heart, if only to protect herself.

Disgusted with himself, he threw his cards down

after one hand. Then he finished his drink and announced that he was in no mood for gambling and was returning to the ballroom.

One of the men at the table laughed and the others nodded knowingly. 'Still in the honeymoon phase,' he said.

'Just restless,' Julian insisted.

'To see your wife,' said another, and the group laughed again.

'Someone's wife,' Julian responded, trying and failing to look as smug as he used to.

The others were having none of his excuses. 'If I had a wife as lovely as yours, I would be on the dance floor as well,' one said. 'Go to her, lad. You don't want to waste your time with us.'

'You are all exceptionally bad company,' Julian said, but the barb had no teeth to it, and the men laughed again and waved him away.

He tried not to hurry on his way back to her, telling himself there was no urgency to the matter. But his steps quickened, and his eyes were scanning the room for Portia before he had even crossed the threshold and was hurrying to her side.

He was in the midst of the group that surrounded her before he'd bothered to look at their faces, for he had eyes only for Portia. When he looked up, he was embarrassed to realise that she was surrounded by his old lovers. Or had she found them, just to annoy him?

Looking at her, she did not seem harassed. Her eyes sparkled as brightly as her jewels, and she was smiling as broadly as any of them. She held out a hand to him, and he took it, clasping it and trying to hide his confusion. 'Julian,' she said, unbothered. 'You have returned.'

'Portia?' He tried to keep the doubt from his voice, glancing around the little circle of women he had known better than he should have.

'We were just talking about you,' she said, still smiling.

'Were you now?' he replied.

The women around her looked as smug as cats in the cream jug. 'It's the job of old married ladies to advise the newest when they join our ranks,' the Countess said smoothly.

'Your friends have been so kind,' Portia said. She was beaming at him, but there was a spark in her eyes that told him they had been anything but.

It was as he'd feared. He had left her to face his past while half of London watched to see how she managed it. But it was not too late to rescue her. 'I have come to claim you for the waltz, as I promised,' he said, offering his hand to her.

'So soon?' she said, inclining her ear towards the orchestra. 'They are playing a reel.'

'I am early then,' he said with a shrug. 'Perhaps we might take a walk around the garden while we wait.'

'How delightful,' she said, and allowed him to escort her from the room.

When they were clear of the crowd and the turns in the garden path obscured them from the house, she glanced in his direction, her smile fading. 'You have a most interesting circle of female friends. What do their husbands think of you?'

'They like me well enough,' he said.

'Better than their wives?'

'In some cases, yes,' he admitted.

'When you bestow your friendship,' she said with a curl of her lip, 'does it ever concern you that someone might be hurt by it?'

'I take care that it is not the case,' he said. 'People I befriend are usually as shallow as I am.'

She said nothing to this for a moment, reaching out to touch one of the flowers on a bush nearby. He stared at her finger, stroking the petals and could imagine her touch.

'You think yourself shallow?' she said quietly.

'I have no illusions about my character,' he said shaking off the distraction. 'I am a creature who lives for pleasure. Little more than that.'

'And yet, you take a seat in Parliament. You attend regularly, do you not?'

'When it is in session,' he said. 'It is my duty to do so.'

'You help craft the laws which govern our country,' she said. 'And the lands that are part of your duchy. Do you manage them well?'

'As well as most,' he said. 'The people seem happy enough.'

'That does not sound the least bit shallow to me,' she said, staring at him.

'When you know me better, you might think differently,' he said, trying to ignore the little swell of undeserved pride that her assessment brought. 'What I did to you tonight was callous of me.'

'Really?' she said, looking away again.

This was the moment when he should apologise and promise that it would not happen again. But he was not in the practice of apologising to anyone when he misbehaved. Not even to himself. He certainly could not guarantee that he would not do something equally awful. It was in his nature to be cruel and contrary.

But in the silence that should have contained those words of regret, he felt small, and when she spoke he felt even smaller.

'In the future, it would be kind of you to give me

some warning when I am about to step into a trap,' she said.

'I will do my best,' he said. He was not in the habit of doing his best either. But for her, perhaps he needed to try.

She smiled at him then, as if the few simple words had healed any breach he'd created. 'Let us go back into the ballroom. I think they are tuning up for the waltz and I do not want to miss it.'

He danced like he made love, possessive and graceful. It was a dangerous experience, for she felt herself forgiving him again, and she was not sure if she really wanted to.

She should not be surprised. He had already proved himself capable of making her do things she had not thought wise.

While they moved around the floor, she felt the eyes of his former lovers upon her, more openly jealous than they had been before. It would be foolish of her to gloat in her success. It was likely as fleeing as theirs had been. But if that was true, she refused to become like them, joining the pack to sneer at the next woman to catch his eye. She must be better than that. Aloof.

That was why, tempting though it was, she must not fall in love with him. She had promised her mother that she would not, and now she promised herself as well.

Then he looked at her and smiled. 'It has been a long evening,' he said. 'If it is not too disappointing to you, I think an early night is in order.' And as he led her to the carriage, still smiling that special smile, she forgot all about her plans to keep her heart safe and followed willingly to the passion that awaited her.

Chapter Fourteen

They made love that night, and the next morning Julian was out of the house when she arose. But a short time later a package was delivered and brought to her in the morning room. When she undid the brown paper wrapping, she found a small, leather case that contained a mother-of-pearl brooch, carved into an ornate heart.

She smiled as she traced the design with her fingertip, then undid the clasp and fixed it at the throat of her gown. It was a token, she supposed, to make up for the embarrassment of the previous evening. Then she remembered Honoria's comment about his mother's jewels and the inferior quality of her own necklace.

She covered the heart with her hand and closed her eyes. It should not matter where he got the thing, so long as he intended it for her. And the shape was significant, she was sure. A gift of his heart, from his heart. While Honoria might scoff, Portia doubted that he'd ever given *her* such a thing. He had been thinking of his wife this morning, and she looked forward to his homecoming and the happy evening they would have together.

But when he came home just after noon, he went straight to his study, not bothering to say hello as he passed the sitting room and slammed the door behind him.

If she'd had stronger nerves, she'd have followed him and asked what the matter was. Clearly, something had changed to make him angry. But if he'd wanted to share it with her, he would have said something, or at least left the door open.

She settled uneasily back into her chair and waited for him to come out. A short time later, he came to stand in the doorway of the sitting room, staring at her until she looked up.

'Portia, if you will accompany me to the study, there is a matter I wish to discuss.'

'Of course,' she said, puzzled. He was behaving as if she had done something wrong, but she had no idea what it could be. She followed him in silence and took the chair in front of his desk, watching as he took his own seat and pushed a pile of papers towards her, then stared at her as if waiting for an explanation.

She looked at them, one after another. There was a bill from a milliner, a modiste, a jewellery store and a shoemaker, all from the same day. She totalled the sums in her head, shocked at the amount, then looked back at him in surprise. 'I do not understand.'

'Neither do I,' he said, staring back, unsmiling. 'Between the gambling winnings and the amount you already took from me, you should have more than enough money for your needs.'

'And you said I should send any bills in excess of it to your bank,' she countered, still staring at the invoices. She hadn't been to any of these places. And she had certainly not gone out to buy herself a ruby necklace. Where had these bills come from?

She looked at the date again. A day after her visit to her mother. Portia had assured her that her worries were over, and all her bills would be paid. She'd intended to do so out of her allowance. But apparently, her mother had taken the initiative to go shopping and use Septon's credit.

'I suppose I should not be surprised,' he said, still staring at her. 'When you proposed this marriage, you made no bones about wanting to enjoy the privileges of my name. It seems you wasted no time in throwing your new title around on Bond Street.'

'I did not...' she began. Then she thought of what he had said about her mother on their wedding day. Perhaps it would be better if he did not know, just yet, that he would be supporting her entire family.

She swallowed. 'Will you honour the bills?'

'I said I would,' he said. 'Despite what you think of me, my word is good.'

'I never...' Did he really assume she thought so little of him? She swallowed again. 'I do not doubt you. I simply thought, since I made you unhappy, you might be rethinking your generosity.'

'I stand by my promise,' he said, sounding tired. 'But in the future, I would prefer that you not hide your expenses from me.'

'I will tell you everything,' she promised, knowing it was a lie, even as she said it.

'That would be best,' he said, glancing to the door as if to tell her that their meeting was over.

'I will go back to the sitting room,' she said. 'If you need me for anything...'

'I will see you at dinner,' he said, gathering up the bills and ignoring her as she left the room.

As the door closed softly behind her, Julian stared down at the expenses his wife had run up in barely two weeks' time. It should not be a surprise, he supposed. They were perfectly ordinary, if somewhat high. But they were nothing he could not afford.

He lifted the jewellery store bill out of the stack, for it puzzled him most of all. Apparently, she'd bought herself a ruby necklace. He felt strange as he stared at the paper, not quite as angry as he had been when his banker had presented him with the whole stack. But indignant. Almost hurt. Weren't his gifts enough for her?

Why, if it had been important enough to buy the thing, had she not bothered to wear it? Her neck had been suspiciously bare in the evenings, except for the topaz set and the pearls she had worn on their wedding day.

He shook his head. It should not surprise him that his wife was a magpie. It was a disappointment, nothing more. Last night, he'd been able to compare her to his old lovers. He'd left the ball wanting to believe that not all women were alike. But his new wife was obviously just as shallow as the rest.

After she was through in the study, Portia went, not to the sitting room as she'd planned, but up to her room to change into a walking gown. She left, hurrying to her mother's house to confirm her suspicions.

When she arrived, her mother was in her bedroom, trying on bonnets and admiring herself in the mirror. She turned, as Portia entered, and gave her a brilliant smile.

Portia greeted her with a stern and disappointed look. 'You have been shopping, again, I see.'

Her mother gave an airy gesture to encompass the

bonnet on her head and a stack of hat boxes on the end of the bed. 'I could not decide what suited me best, so I got several.' She smiled at the pile of clothes beside the boxes. 'And gowns as well.'

'Where did you get the money for such expenses?' she said, praying that there could be any other explanation.

'From your husband, of course,' her mother said, showing no shame.

'What right did you have to do so?' Portia said, staring at the new gowns in dismay.

'We are family now,' she replied, her eyes narrowing slightly. 'I did not think I needed permission.'

'But you could have asked for it, all the same,' she said, then grasped at a compromise. 'We could have gone shopping together.'

'I did not want to bother you,' her mother said. But there was something about her tone, and her evasive gaze that made Portia wonder if it was a lie. 'And you had said that you would visit me soon.'

'I am here now,' she said, embarrassed to have forgotten her promise. 'I should have come before. Julian is out of the house most days, and there is very little I need to do.'

'He is leaving you alone already, is he?' her mother said, pouncing like a cat on anything that would show her husband in a poor light.

'Not alone. He has been most attentive so far,' she said, trying not to think of his Wednesday appointments. 'And very generous.'

'As well he should be,' her mother said with a nod.

'But that does not mean that you are free to use his money for spending sprees on Bond Street.'

'I thought that was the reason you married him,' her mother countered. 'So that we could afford to live in comfort.'

'Well, yes,' Portia agreed. It had been her plan when she had first gone to him. But things had grown much more complicated since then. 'We all need time to adjust to our new circumstances,' she said. 'And at the wedding, you did not make the best impression on him.'

'You married a rake, but you are blaming me for the difficulties you have?' her mother said with an exaggerated gesture of shock.

'Of course not,' she said quickly. 'But I have not had a chance to discuss our future with Julian. I am hoping that he will be willing to give you an allowance of some kind. And he will need to see your household accounts…'

Her mother let out a hiss of disapproval.

She ignored it and pushed on. 'Until I do, I would prefer that you not try his patience with excessive spending.'

'My spending was in no way excessive,' her mother insisted. 'I have not had a new ballgown in ages.'

'We each got new wardrobes at the beginning of the season. I just settled the bills for them.' she said, thinking of the expense she had still not explained. 'And you did not need to buy jewellery.'

'You do not want me to shame you when we are seen together by being unfashionable,' her mother said.

'Well, now you have everything you need,' Portia, said, staring at the bonnets and bandboxes that surrounded them.

'For now,' her mother said with a secretive smile.

Had she always been thus, or was it Portia's marriage that had brought this avaricious streak to the surface? If this were her true nature, it might explain her father's behaviour and all the arguments she had overheard. 'No more shopping until I have talked to Julian,' she said in a firm tone and rose to go.

'Of course not, dear,' her mother agreed. But there was something in her expression that hinted this would not be the last of the problems she created.

That night, when she came into dinner, Portia looked thoroughly contrite. There was still no sign of the ruby necklace, which made Julian wonder if he had frightened her off wearing it. Instead, she wore the little brooch he had bought that morning. It was hardly appropriate for a dinner gown, but he was pleased to see it, all the same.

She touched it as she sat down, to be sure he had noticed. 'I did not thank you for this earlier,' she said with a smile.

'It was nothing,' he said. In truth, it was very little. But it eased some of the guilt for the embarrassment of the previous evening.

'And there will be no more surprise bills,' she promised. Then her smile faltered. 'Save for one,' she added giving him a nervous glance, then staring back at her plate.

'And what would that be for?' he asked.

'I need more evening clothes,' she said in a small voice. 'I had but one gown made for the Belleville ball. But I have accepted other invitations. The Glenmoor party. The Felkirk ball.' She shrugged. 'I did not think.'

He stared at her in surprise. If she was shopping again, what had become of the gowns she had just purchased? But this time, she was coming to him beforehand and seemed so apologetic that it was hard to be angry with her. 'Very well. I will expect it. In the future, I would prefer that you tell me of these things instead of letting my banker surprise me.'

'I will,' she said, obviously relieved. There was a

long pause, before she said, 'When I lived with my mother, there was never enough money for such purchases. For either of us.'

'You have alluded to that,' he said, serving her a slice of beef.

'She is still in constrained circumstances,' she said. 'It is of much concern to me.'

This was a hint, he supposed, that it was his duty to care for the woman. 'Does she still loathe me?' he asked, refusing to make the conversation an easy one.

'She does not loathe you,' Portia said, attempting a dismissive laugh.

'Is that so?' he said, slicing another piece of the roast and placing it on his own plate.

'She is simply having a difficult time with the loss of me,' she said.

'Then you must visit her and assure her that you have not died,' he said. 'You have married, just as you both planned that you should.'

'I spoke to her only today,' she said, giving him a brilliant smile. 'I told her how well things were going. And how happy we...' She paused again. 'I am.' Now, she was waiting for reassurance from him.

He thought of the debts of hers he had paid today and did not bother looking up. 'Things are going as I expected them to,' he said, taking a drink of wine.

'Perhaps, if we were to have her to dinner,' she said.

He could feel her smile, bearing down on him like a lead weight.

'My opinion on the matter will not change,' he said, 'until hers has.' He looked up then, directly into her eyes. 'There is a limit to what you can expect when you marry a man with no respect for society's rules. Supporting a woman who wants no part of me is over the line.'

'Of course,' she said quietly and changed the subject.

Chapter Fifteen

Several days had passed since her abortive attempt to persuade her husband to care for her mother. Since that unfortunate dinner, Portia was at a loss as to how to proceed. She had gone to her mother again, during the day, hoping to soften her view of Julian, but the woman was intractable.

'So he doesn't want to care for me,' her mother had said. 'It is not a surprise to find that he is a tight-fisted scoundrel. His sort cannot be trusted to live up to their responsibilities. Just look at your father, God rest his soul.'

'Perhaps, if you did not compare him to others,' Portia begged.

'He and your father were two peas in a pod,' she insisted. 'I compare them because they are the same.' She would not budge from that position, no matter what Portia said.

She came home again, disheartened. Her mother

could manage without help for a while, now that the outstanding debts were paid. But if she could not move Julian to handle the matter, she would have to take more money from the box in the study, the next time Mother ran short of funds. Or perhaps, she could persuade him to set an allowance for her and she could take the money from that. Really, she did not need much for herself, if she knew that things were all right at home.

But tonight, she was going with Julian to a party at the home of the Duke and Duchess of Belston, which she hoped would be easier than their last outing. Her husband could not promise her that she wouldn't meet any more of his old lovers, but he assured her that he had never lain with the hostess. It was something, she supposed.

When they arrived at the Belston townhouse the Duchess, who was a rather plain woman with thick spectacles, smiled at Julian and said, 'It is so nice to have you in our home, now that you are properly married and no longer a menace to my female guests.'

'A menace?' Julian said with a self-deprecating gesture. 'I was never that. A gift, perhaps, but never a menace.'

The Duchess laughed and looked at Portia with a conspiratorial smile. 'I am only teasing. We adore your husband. Everyone does.'

'I have noticed,' Portia said with an exasperated smile.

'It is nice to meet you as well,' the Duchess said, giving her hand a friendly squeeze. 'I have found that reformed rakes make the best husbands, and I am sure the two of you will be very happy.'

Portia fought the urge to announce that her husband had done nothing to mend his character and accepted the compliment with as much grace as she could manage.

They were led to a sitting room where the other guests waited before the call came to go in to dinner. There were many people there that Portia had not yet met, and she was relieved to see that only one of Julian's former inamoratas was present. The Duchess of Belleville was there, unaccompanied by her husband.

Portia had seen little of him at the ball they'd attended, which made her wonder if things were as Julian said, and the woman's husband truly was not interested in where she went or who she associated with. Their hostess must have known something of their past for, when they took their places at table, Portia discovered that Honoria had been seated far down the table from Julian, where there would be no chance for her to cause trouble.

She took her assigned seat, across the table from Julian and was able to relax and enjoy the dinner. The gentlemen on either side of her made pleasant conversation, and the table was heavily laden with dishes to tempt any palate.

When the meal was finished, the ladies withdrew to the drawing room while the men were still taking port in the dining room. To entertain them for the rest of the evening, the Duchess had set up tables for cards and backgammon and arranged for coffee and tea to be served. Unlike the Belleville ball, which had been stressful and unpleasant, Portia was having a wonderful time and looked forward to becoming more acquainted with their hostess, whose name was Penelope.

Only one thing, or rather one person, marred the happiness of the evening. Honoria made no effort to corner Portia, as she had at the ball, but she was still there, in the same room, smiling her venomous smile and trying to make Portia feel as if she did not belong. There was nothing to do but ignore her, and Portia made a point of staying on the opposite side of the room, focusing on the conversations nearest to her.

She was so successful in this that she did not notice when the Duchess of Belleville left the room. She was probably just answering a call of nature, and there was no reason to be concerned. But, as the minutes ticked by and she did not reappear, Portia grew more and more nervous. Seeing the woman had been bad enough. But things were even worse when she did not know what Honoria might be up to.

Eventually Portia could stand it no longer, and made her apologies, then left the room to go in search of her.

As he was enjoying his port, Julian silently congratulated himself on how well the evening had gone. It was none of his doing, of course. His only contribution to the success had been agreeing to marry Portia. Tonight she was proving that she could be an asset to him in ways he'd never expected.

He had been surprised when she'd told him that they had received an invitation from Belston's wife, as he'd never run in the same set as the Duke. That man had a scandalous past of his own but was viewed as one of the great political minds of the age. In comparison, Julian was a rank beginner in Parliament and had so far had little success in getting his ideas heard or acted upon.

But their wives had taken to each other on this first meeting and would likely seek each other out once this party was done. Portia had made good impressions at dinner as well, charming the men on either side of her and chatting amiably with their wives in the drawing room beforehand. In turn, those men treated Julian with greater respect than usual as they'd shared their after-dinner port.

He was used to acting the fool and being treated as such: a man of superior rank but superficial ideas. But tonight, he was a man amongst equals. The whole evening seemed right in a way he was not familiar with.

It would be even better when the gentlemen joined their wives again so they might begin the evening's entertainment. Though he enjoyed the serious conversation of men, he wanted to see Portia again, just to know that she was faring well. When the time came to go to the drawing room, he was the first to excuse himself and seek them out.

He should have waited for his host. Though he had been in the drawing room just an hour before, he made a wrong turning in the hallway and found himself standing in the darkened library and not where he should be. It was just as well, he supposed. If he rushed to be with her, the other gentlemen would say he was hanging on his wife's skirts, and he would be a laughingstock at the club tomorrow.

But dammit, she looked delicious tonight, her eyes sparkling with happiness as she chatted with the people around her and exclaimed in pleasure at the elegance of the dishes served. The sight of her raised a strange, unfamiliar feeling in him. He had been eager for each passing glance she'd spared him from across the table. He'd been tempted to slight his own partners and insist that she talk to him, even though they had all the time in the world to speak when they were not out in company.

Was this jealousy?

He smiled in surprise. It was not something he'd experienced before. In the past, his attention had waned long before he'd had any serious feelings for the women he was with. But tonight, he was looking forward to being with her, counting the minutes until they could be alone again.

How long would this go on? *Not much longer*, he thought. It was not as if he could spend his life besotted with her. That sort of love was the stuff of myth. If he found his own company tiring, how could he feel eternal love for someone else?

He walked out of the room and made to shut the door only to find Honoria walking slowly towards him, blocking his way back to the party.

A wave of ennui smothered the anticipation he had been feeling. His affair with the Duchess had been over a Season ago, brief and pleasant but nothing he cared to revisit.

She was looking at him now as if she expected the spark to rekindle at her suggestion. 'Julian,' she cooed, coming to a stop only inches from him, standing too close to be proper. 'Were you looking for me?'

'For a chamber pot, actually,' he said with a firm smile. 'And privacy.'

She laughed, refusing to take the hint and move on. 'Well, you have found me instead. Perhaps we can find privacy together.' She reached out a hand and laid it on his chest, just over his heart.

If she was hoping to hear the beat increase, she would be disappointed. He felt nothing but irritation. He made no effort to touch her in return. 'That rather defeats the purpose of being alone, Honoria. And I doubt my wife would approve of me running off to be with you while I am still on my honeymoon.'

At this, she laughed even harder, a smug sound in the silence of the hall. 'Then we will not tell her. Really, Julian, it's as if you have forgotten how these things are done.'

'Perhaps it is time I forgot,' he said, taking a step back into the darkened room behind him.

Honoria paid no attention, closing the distance between them again. 'Now you sound like an old man, and you are nothing of the sort.'

'Not much older. But marriage has made me wiser,' he said, wondering what he had ever seen in her.

'I hardly think that is likely,' she said with a condescending smile. 'You will be the same rogue you always have been by the time the orange blossoms have wilted.'

'But not with you,' he said bluntly, taking another step back.

Her smile faded a little, but she took a step towards him again. 'You cannot mean that you plan to be faithful to that naive little chit you have married.'

'I said nothing of the kind,' he replied. 'But that doesn't mean that I wish to make a fool of myself just days after my wedding.'

'Then why are you luring me into the darkness?' she said with a laugh.

Behind her, there was a feminine gasp of shock, and the sound of something hitting the marble floor.

He pushed past Honoria and out into the hall to see who had caught them. Portia was frozen in shock and standing a few feet from them. Had she heard his denial? Probably not, for her face was white and the fan that she had dropped still lay at her feet.

Honoria's hand still rested on his lapel, and he was sure if he turned back to her he would see an expression of possessive triumph on her face. She had achieved what she'd wanted from the first, even more than she wanted him. She had wrenched a response from the unflappable Portia.

This is nothing.

He should say it, because what she had witnessed was indeed innocent, at least compared to a lifetime of flagrant disregard for society morals. But for some reason, the words stuck in his throat.

Would she believe them anyway? In his experience,

women believed what they wanted to, no matter what the truth. And it should not matter in any case because she had promised that she would not care, no matter what he did.

But there was something in her eyes that said that was a lie. She cared very much. More than that, she was hurting. He stared at her in silence, fascinated. He could relieve that pain, if he wanted to.

If he wanted to.

But some horrible part of him revelled in this small revelation. She cared. He was still afraid to discover that there was anything beneath the glittering, gold surface of her. Yet this indiscretion had clearly struck her to the heart.

Then she turned without another word and went back down the hall, as if nothing had happened.

He felt Honoria's hand tugging at his coat. 'And now, after that small interruption, let us go into the library and return to our conversation.'

He reached out and disentangled her fingers from his coat. Her hand, which had always felt so soft in his, felt like the claw of some predatory animal. 'I believe we were done, Honoria. I have nothing more to say to you.'

'Tonight, perhaps,' she said, still smiling. 'But when you grow tired of domestication, you know where to find me.'

He released her hand, thrusting it away from him. 'You presume too much, Honoria. What was between us was sweet while it lasted. But it was a brief interlude. It will not ever be repeated.'

Her eyes narrowed and her smile grew hard. 'You really are a bastard, Julian.'

'I never claimed to be anything else,' he said simply. Then he turned from her and stooped to collect his wife's fan before going in search of her.

Chapter Sixteen

Portia stepped into the first open room before returning to the drawing room, fussing with her hem and trying to pretend that she was merely fatigued and not near to frustrated tears. It had been less upsetting to follow her husband into dens of iniquity, fully prepared to be shocked by his actions than it was to catch him straying when they were out in polite society.

Despite the jokes she'd heard earlier, she had not imagined that his bad behaviour would follow them to respectable parties, or that at any time he might be sneaking off for an assignation with one of the women she would be forced to call friends.

And to be able to say nothing to any of it? The humiliation of having to ignore his indiscretions when he rubbed them in her face was more than she could bear. Her mother had been right all along. He would break her heart and not think twice about it.

She glanced in a nearby mirror, gauging the damage. She looked wan. It didn't matter if she looked dreadful, she could not hide here all night. She must return to the party and smile through Julian's absence so that no one suspected there was a problem.

She reached up to pinch some colour into her cheeks, then stopped. It would only make the situation worse, creating bright pink splotches where her fingers had been. Instead, she balled her hands into fists and opened her mouth to inhale a gasp and exhale a silent scream.

She looked into the mirror again, pleased to see that her colour had returned. She bared her teeth for a moment, then settled her mouth into a polite smile. Turning her head from side to side, she gently patted her hair into place, then left the room to return to the party.

When she arrived in the drawing room, Julian was there, waiting for her, smiling as if nothing had happened. He reached into a coat pocket and withdrew her fan, handing it back to her without explanation.

She wanted to scream aloud this time. To tell him what she thought of him and the harridan he could not seem to keep away from. Instead, she took the fan with a smile, snapped it open and waved it vigorously. She offered a nod of gratitude and looked past him to the gaming tables.

Out of the corner of her eye, she watched his expression falter. The smooth, society smile disappeared, replaced with confusion and... Could it be anger? He had wanted her to be hurt and was disappointed that she was not. Was that it?

All the more reason for her to show nothing of her true feelings. She could not give him the satisfaction of success, or he would pull similar tricks every time they went out.

Across the room, Honoria was waving her own fan, trying to lure Julian to the empty seat at her side.

It was too easy.

Portia deliberately misunderstood her, and with a small squeal of delight, hurried to her and took the empty chair. 'Honoria,' she said, in a voice brimming with honey and sunshine. 'We have not spoken all evening. We must play together.'

'Must we?' she responded, shooting Julian a desperate look which he sensibly ignored.

'Definitely,' Portia said, shuffling the cards and eyeing her opponents. The other two seats were occupied by a bishop's wife, who she suspected would be no competition at all, and Penelope, who had hurried to take the last chair when she saw that Portia meant to sit beside her husband's lover.

Portia smiled at her, offering silent assurance that there would be no hair pulling or screaming like fishwives. Just cards. Cards would be enough.

'Quadrille,' she suggested, sorting the deck before anyone could refuse. 'Let us play for pennies, just to make it interesting.'

'I never play for stakes so small,' Honoria said with a sniff.

'Pounds then,' Portia said with a smile.

The bishop's wife looked alarmed, peering into her empty reticule.

'Do not worry,' Portia said, pushing her a pile of the mother-of-pearl fish they were using as counters. 'I will stake you. It is only for fun, after all.'

Play began and Portia forgot her anger, too focused on the challenge she set for herself. She wanted to win, of course. But not at the expense of everyone at the table. She discarded carefully and formed alliances when she could, splitting the pool with the bishop's wife on several occasions and making the woman laugh at her own success. Penelope was smart enough that she needed no help to win a few games of her own.

But to Honoria, Portia was merciless. The other duchess was a foolish player, always losing track of trump and clueless as to the strategy of the women playing against her. In no time, she had lost the counters in front of her and, by the set of her jaw, she had nothing in her reticule to purchase more.

'Here,' Portia said, pushing a pile of fish in her direction. 'I trust your marker is good.'

'Of course,' Honoria said through gritted teeth and continued to play.

They had played for nearly two hours before Julian appeared at her shoulder. 'I think we have had enough fun for the evening.'

'Yes,' Honoria said, answering for her in a flat voice. 'It has been delightful.'

The bishop's wife pushed the pile of fish towards her side of the table, and Portia picked out the ten she had offered as a stake, then pushed the rest back. 'You must keep your winnings, of course. They belong to you.' Then she turned to Honoria. 'And you can settle your debt to me whenever you like. I am in no hurry.'

'How gracious of you,' Honoria replied, staring daggers.

After thanking her hostess for a lovely evening, she walked with Julian to their carriage, settling into her seat, smiling smugly into the darkness and in no mood to talk to him.

After they'd ridden several miles in silence, he spoke. 'How much?'

'Fifty pounds,' she replied.

'Did you enjoy yourself?' He had the nerve to sound annoyed.

'Oh, yes,' she said, still smiling. 'It was the best time I've had in ages.'

When, at last, they arrived at the townhouse, he escorted her up the stairs to their rooms and said, in the same irritated voice, 'You are tired. I will leave you to your rest.'

Then he went to his room and she was alone with her maid.

As Rose prepared her for bed, Portia stared at the door connecting their rooms, her anger returning. It was clear that he did not wish to speak of what had occurred at the party. But that did not mean it hadn't happened.

Did he think she would forget, just because she had promised not to care? She would be a fool to do so.

She climbed into bed and stared up at the canopy above her, wide awake, thinking of things she wished to say to him, running the lines over and over in her head like an actor learning the words to their part.

For good measure, she played his role as well, imagining each argument he might make in response. Would he tell her that she had not seen what she'd seen?

There was nothing wrong with her vision, so that was nonsense.

Would he tell her that it was an inconsequential flirtation?

Then she would ask him why such an unimportant thing had to occur under her very nose and not on an evening when she did not accompany him.

But she would not stand by mute and let this pass. When she saw him, tomorrow…

Then she remembered that it was Tuesday evening. Tomorrow would be Wednesday again.

The next day, Julian was out of the house early, as he always was when he slept at home. But this day was different. He needed to do something to make up for the embarrassment of the previous evening. He had gone to bed with a book instead of in the arms of his wife, as he had been in no mood to kiss her after her behaviour at Belston's.

Her response to catching him with Honoria had been perfect. She had behaved just as she'd promised and proved to him that he could do just as he liked, with no repercussions. After that one brief gasp of surprise, she had returned to the party without turning a hair.

An ordinary woman, the sort who married for love, would have brained him with the fan when he returned it to her and stormed from the room. Then, at least, he'd have known she cared.

But his wife had spent the evening bankrupting

Honoria. It had been the sort of civilised response that was expected from a lady of the *ton*.

He could not help a small smile at the memory of Honoria's expression when Portia had taken the seat intended for him. That had been a masterstroke.

She had behaved just as he would have hoped. And in response, he had been cross with her. He was cross with himself as well. He'd meant to be on his best behaviour, last night, if only to show respect to his host and hostess. Instead, he'd been stupid enough to be trapped by Honoria, who was seeking a liaison that would have embarrassed them both. If they'd been alone together for any length of time, the whole party would have noticed their absence and drawn the obvious conclusion.

But only Portia had suspected. And the way she'd handled the situation like a sophisticated woman of the world was exemplary. He could not ask for a better wife. He had no right to expect a show of temper or to be hurt by her indifference. Jealousy was not part of their bargain, any more than love was. He should not be wishing for a thing that would only cause trouble. Last night he'd been in the wrong, and she deserved…

Something that proved he was aware of his mistake. A token like the little brooch he'd given her after the last encounter with Honoria. But this time, it should be something more significant. This situation called for diamonds.

Since he had plans later in the day, instead of boxing or riding or any of the other vigorous exercises he normally did in the morning, he was the first customer at Garrard's jewellery shop and came away with a diamond bracelet guaranteed to set things right between them.

Then he went back to the townhouse and straight to her room. He let himself in through the hall door, surprising the maid and waving her away before going to the dressing table and arranging the little leather box on top of it. As he stared down at his handiwork, he heard a faint rustling of the bedclothes behind him and the rattle of the curtain rings as she moved the hangings out of the way to peer at him.

He smiled and pretended not to notice, opening the jewel case to display the bracelet to good effect. Then he turned, pretending to ignore the bed and moving towards the door to let himself out so he could be on his way.

There was a bustle of activity behind him as she hurried to see what he had left for her.

He paused in the doorway, waiting to feel the body pelting into him, the caress of pleased surprise, the sigh of satisfaction and gratitude…

Instead, to his complete shock, something that felt

like a leather jewel box hit him square in the middle of his back.

When he turned, she was standing by the dressing table in charming dishabille, simmering with rage, her hands balled at her side and her expression grim.

'How dare you?' she spat, practically levitating in anger.

'What did I do?' he asked, baffled.

'Nothing,' she said. 'Nothing at all.'

'Then why are you so angry?' Her response made no sense. Nor did refusing a gift that any woman of his acquaintance would be proud to wear.

'Because I am a fool,' she said, and seemed to calm somewhat.

He considered this for a moment, but it did not enlighten him. If she was angry with herself, then why was he bearing the brunt of it?

She was staring at him now, still fuming, and he was convinced that there was something he must say but still unsure as to what it might be. 'About last night,' he began.

Her eyes narrowed almost imperceptibly but she said nothing.

'I did not lure Honoria into that hallway, if that is what you are thinking. She followed me.'

'Then why are you buying me jewellery?' she demanded.

'Because...' Why indeed? Because it was easier than talking. It explained why his father had spent so much on diamonds over the years, since his parents had rarely spoken at all. 'I thought you wanted it?' His answer had come out like a question. He did not like sounding unsure.

'Not if you mean to give me something each time you do something despicable.'

'I did nothing despicable,' he said, incensed. 'I turned her down. I had no intention of meeting her when I left the dining room. As I said before, she was the one who searched me out.'

Portia stared at him, disgusted. 'Then why did you not say something sooner?'

He had no good answer for that. Perhaps it was because he had hoped she would trust him. But when had he ever given her a reason to do so?

Then he remembered their agreement. 'Why do you even care?'

She sputtered for a moment, then regrouped. 'And why, since everyone tells me of the fabulous Septon jewels, do you not give me any of them? Why do you insist on buying me more?'

Was that what this was about? Was she so eager to get her hands on the contents of his mother's jewel case? The memory of them made him as sick as her desire for them did. 'Perhaps you have not yet earned the right to wear my mother's jewels,' he replied coolly.

Or perhaps she had. Each one of his mother's pieces had been given out of his father's guilt for some sin or other. And now, though he had never wanted to become his father, he was playing the same game.

She reached down to touch the opal betrothal ring she still wore on her right hand. She twisted it off and threw it at him, as she had the bracelet.

He caught it in his clenched fist as she said, 'Then I suppose you should have this back. It is not as if we are betrothed any more. I have the wedding ring you bought for me. Would you like that as well?' She pulled it off and held it out to him.

He stared at it, confused. He had wanted to hurt her for refusing his gift. But hadn't he already hurt her by speaking with Honoria? That had not been his fault. But still...

'Keep it,' he said. 'And this as well.' He held the betrothal ring out to her.

She stared at it in suspicion.

'I should not have said what I just did,' he admitted.

She took the ring from his hand and slipped it on her finger again. Then she looked down at the bracelet she had thrown at him, which had spilled from its case and was lying on the floor. 'You can take that back to wherever it came from,' she said, refusing to meet his eyes. 'You do not need to buy me gifts. Marrying me was sufficient.'

He was about to snap that he would buy her whatever he chose to, and she had damn well better wear it. But she looked sad, as if accepting the bracelet was some sort of punishment he was heaping on her, along with the embarrassment of the Honoria incident.

'Very well,' he said, planning to lock it in his desk in the study. To return it after less than a day would be almost as embarrassing as her refusal. He turned to go.

Before he could reach the door of her room, she called him back. 'Wait.'

He turned to her, saying nothing.

'Will you be home for supper?' she asked.

'Do not wait up,' he said, and left.

As Julian left her, Portia reached to touch her betrothal ring again, twisting it nervously on her finger. It was some consolation, she supposed, to know that he had not intended to meet Honoria last night. He had insisted it was an innocent mistake and she believed him. When he bothered to tell her anything at all, he bragged about his sins rather than hiding them. If he'd meant to meet Honoria, he'd have done it in daylight, just as he was meeting his lover today.

That did not explain why he could not have simply explained it all to her last night. And though she had thought the evening had gone well and his friends had accepted her, this morning he had said the thing that she most feared: that he did not think her worthy to be his wife. He was refusing to bestow on her the family jewels to demonstrate to the world what he thought of her.

Today he had tried to placate her with a hastily bought trinket, and before that the brooch and the topaz parure. They suited her well, though they were not as valuable as some sets might have been. But money was not the point. It was the meaning of the things that mattered. If he was selecting pieces that had no history, perhaps she meant nothing to him as well.

As if to prove her theory, he had tried to give her a gift this morning and then gone directly to the arms of another woman. It did not matter how many times she told herself not to care. She still hurt when she thought about the beautiful girl in St John's Woods.

She summoned Rose and washed and dressed, then went downstairs to begin her day. As she passed through the foyer, Banks greeted her with a subtle incline of his head and a worried look.

She answered with a weak smile and went in to breakfast alone, because she had no choice. But was that true? She knew her husband would be gone on Wednesdays. That was his choice. Why did she have to keep reminding herself that she need not sit in an empty house, mourning his loss?

She had no desire to shop, nor was she eager to pay any morning calls. But perhaps there was something she could do in the evening that would fill the difficult hours between supper and midnight. She set her breakfast aside and went into the morning room, where she kept the week's post, shuffling through the invitations she'd received until she found one she had previously discarded.

Tonight, there was to be a ball at the residence of Lady Mary Hackville and her daughters. She had already sent regrets, knowing that Julian would be away from home. But when they'd married, she had made no vow that they be joined at the hip for such outings.

It was rather late to change her mind, of course. But this was nothing as intimate as a dinner party. There should be room for an additional guest at such a large gathering. Or, perhaps two. If she was going to be so rude as to change her mind about attending, she might as well bring her mother instead of Julian. Mother had scolded her for keeping her distance the last time she'd visited. She would probably enjoy an evening out.

She sat down to scribble a fresh reply to Lady Mary and summoned a footman to deliver it directly and await an answer from the hostess. In no time at all, she received an affirmative message that the Hackvilles would be honoured to have Her Grace and Mrs Braddock this evening for dancing and a buffet supper.

She smiled, thinking the solution was by far the best one she'd come up with. Julian had said she should not wait up for him and she was following his instructions. She might be up until dawn, but instead of lying in bed wondering where he might be, she would show both him and the *ton* that she was perfectly happy with things as they were.

Since Lord Hackville was only a baron, she doubted that she would meet Julian's crop of gossiping former lovers. By the speed of Lady Mary's response, she suspected she might be the highest-ranking lady there. If people whispered about her sudden marriage to Septon or wondered if he was in the arms of a woman who was not his wife, at least they would not do it to her face, as Honoria might.

She wrote to her mother to tell her of the plan, then left the morning room and went to find Banks, informing him of her intentions and her need for the carriage at eight that evening.

'Of course, Your Grace,' the butler said, giving her a look that implied he did not like the idea at all.

'Is there some problem?' she asked fixing him with an unyielding stare.

'His Grace often requires the carriage on Wednesday evenings,' he said, looking unhappy about that as well.

She thought for a moment. 'Tell the coachman that, since His Grace enjoys exercise, he can partake of it this evening on his way home from St John's Wood.' Then she went to her room to take a nap so she might be rested for the long night ahead.

Chapter Seventeen

They were just finishing supper when a footman arrived from Septon House with a message for Julian. He snapped the seal on it, surprised to see Banks's efficient script explaining that the carriage would be needed by Her Grace this evening and wondering whether he wished a hired equipage to wait for him or if perhaps he preferred to walk.

If he was proceeding on foot, did he wish a link boy to light the way, or would the footman be sufficient escort?

Julian frowned down at the note. It was annoying on so many levels. When he'd left the house, Portia had no plans that he was aware of. Why had she waited until now to inform him? Why had she left the notification to Banks?

And why the devil was Banks going on about footman and link boys when he knew Julian was accustomed to walking alone and in the dark without complaint? It was a surprise the butler had not suggested he be carried home in a sedan chair like an old lady or an invalid.

'What is the matter?' Cassandra looked at him over the rim of her wine glass, smiling as if his irritation amused her.

'My wife has commandeered my transport,' he said with a scowl.

'Good for her,' she replied, offering a toast to the absent woman. 'It is most unfair of you to neglect her. You have barely been together a month.'

'I did not ask for your opinion,' he said, turning his chair so he could throw the note into the fire.

'Then you can consider yourself lucky that I have gifted you with it,' she said, still smiling.

'It appears we must make an early night of it, since I will be walking home,' he said, rising from the table and looking with regret at the bottle of his favourite port, which was waiting on the sideboard.

'There is always next week,' she reminded him.

'True enough,' he said with a sigh. 'And I must go to see what trouble she is up to now. The woman cannot be trusted out alone.'

His hostess laughed. 'Then she is probably a good match for you. Go to her.' She led him to the front door and sent him off into the darkness with a kiss on the cheek, far less bothered with the interruption than he was.

Of course, she did not have to walk two miles in the dark.

By the time he arrived at home, he was thoroughly vexed with Portia for spoiling his plans and with himself for not hiring a carriage as Banks had suggested. As usual, the butler was waiting at the door for him and greeted him with a subdued smirk, as if enjoying the discomfort his master had been put through.

'Where is she, Banks?' he said, offering no further explanation. 'And do not tell me you do not know. You are fully aware of everything that happens in this house, and I am in no mood to play games.'

'I believe she sent a response to Lady Hackville about the ball this evening,' the butler said after a moment's thought.

'Hackville,' Julian repeated.

'On Finsbury Square,' the butler supplied. 'Do you wish me to hire a coach?'

'I will walk,' Julian said through gritted teeth.

'Shall I tell Mason to lay out your evening clothes?'

'Evening clothes be damned!' Julian barked, setting his hat back on his head and striking out on foot to find his wife.

As they arrived at the Hackville ball, Portia was already beginning to regret her decision to come. Since her marriage, something had changed between her mother and herself. Their interactions had become difficult because they could not seem to agree on anything. When she had been seeking a husband, she had looked to her mother for advice on how best to present herself to attract the attention of the young men who courted her.

But now she was married and a duchess as well. Her mother could not help her with the etiquette for the latter. And as for the former? Portia was beginning to question the soundness of her advice on marriage as well. She and father had not been happy together. If she'd behaved to Father as she did to Julian? Portia could not blame him for staying away from home.

'It is a shame that the Duke has abandoned you,' her mother announced as they neared the door of the Hackville townhouse.

'He did not abandon me,' Portia said, struggling to keep her composure. 'He had other plans, that is all.'

'Of course, dear,' her mother said with a pitying sigh.

'I asked you to accompany me because I thought you would enjoy it,' Portia reminded her. 'But if you mean to spread gossip about me, there will be no such invitations in the future.'

'Gossip?' she said with wide eyes and a flutter of her fan.

'Certainly not.'

'Lady Mary is gaining quite a reputation for her entertainments,' Portia reminded her. 'I hear she has hired an artist to chalk the ballroom floor. It is good that we have arrived early so we might see the design before the dancing has begun.'

The prospect of seeing such a novel decoration so distracted her mother that she forgot all about her need to defame Julian to anyone who would listen. Portia was fascinated as well to see the drawing of an elaborate Turkish carpet done in reds and purples and golds, stretching from one wall to the other. It had been put there for no reason other than to enhance the flower arrangements and provide a little traction for leather slippers on a smooth wood floor.

Once they had greeted their hostess, Portia tied a dance card around her wrist and agreed to stand up with several gentlemen who she'd met earlier in the Season. She also had the opportunity to converse happily with old friends that she had not seen since her marriage. The company here was not so grand as Julian might have preferred, but it suited Portia well, and she hoped for a pleasant evening, untroubled by thoughts of her husband's former or current lovers.

It was going almost too well. Until a crowd of laughing men came back from the card room and dispersed to reveal the Duke of Westbridge standing in their midst.

Portia turned away quickly, pretending that she had not seen him. But she could not resist staring into the mirror near the main ballroom doors and caught his reflection as he accepted a glass of champagne and leaned against the far wall of the room. He was paler than she remembered, and his left arm was tied up with a black silk sling. He was as devilishly handsome as ever with wavy blonde hair and a smile that hinted he knew far too much.

She scanned the room for her mother, wondering if it would be possible to pull her away from her friends and exit discreetly before he noticed her. If she did not want to incite gossip, she should not be in the same place as Westbridge, much less speak to him. The scandal of the duel was still too fresh in the minds of the *ton*.

But was that really fair? She'd done nothing to encourage the Duke. And she'd had to face far worse when she'd met Honoria and her friends.

But Julian had been with her when that had happened, a reminder to all that she had already won the game the other ladies wished to play. Tonight, she was alone and Julian had no knowledge of her plans. Suppose he heard of this meeting and thought it was deliberate? She would have to explain it to him before he read of it in the papers.

Assuming she saw him in time. He had always been

at home on Thursday after his Wednesday outings. But could one trust in *always* after only a month? Their marriage was far too new to count on anything. They had argued this morning and she'd been deliberately provoking when she had taken the carriage away from him. If she did not want to cause further trouble, she should leave now.

But before she could make a move towards the door, a new guest appeared. Julian was here, in a day coat and boots, looking the worse for wear after what had probably been a long walk in the dark. He also looked very angry.

She raised her fan to hide her face and fluttered it furiously. Then more slowly, so as not to call attention to herself. He would see her soon enough, but she needed time to think. She should compose herself and go to greet him as if nothing was wrong. Because nothing *was* wrong. He had encouraged her to accept invitations and placed no restrictions on her socialising. The fact that Westbridge was here was merely an unfortunate coincidence.

Then, if possible, things became even worse. Her mother had noticed him and was glaring in his direction, eager for a confrontation. She was also wearing the necklace and gown she'd bought with money she had all but stolen from him. How closely had he read the bills, she wondered? Were men in the habit of noticing that they'd paid for crimson sarcenet and gold braid?

He was barely through the door before her mother waved off her friends and moved to accost him, taking him by the arm and turning to face him as she talked.

Portia searched the mirror by the door, trying to catch sight of her and guess the gist of the conversation. But the shorter woman was hidden by her tall husband's forbiddingly rigid back. He did not look very welcoming from the front either. His brows were knit, his expression stormy and his end of the conversation was delivered through lips set in a frown.

She should stop this. Even if Julian remained civil, she could not trust her mother to be so, especially after a few glasses of wine. She needed to do something, but to walk into their midst was likely to cause an even bigger argument, right in the doorway.

She turned and glanced behind her, looking for escape and saw nothing but Westbridge, who noticed her and smiled, raising his glass in salute.

For a moment, she had no idea where she should focus. Her gaze swung between the two sides of the room. She was trapped between Scylla and Charybdis. There would be trouble either way.

She covered her mouth with her fan, trying to contain the mad laughter that was bubbling up inside her.

If the night was to end in disaster, it might as well be the biggest one possible.

She lowered her fan and waved it madly until she was sure she'd caught Julian's attention. Then she turned and walked to greet his enemy.

By his estimation, when Julian arrived at the ball he'd walked almost six miles through the darkened streets of London. The whole way, he'd been thinking of what he wished to say to his wife. Most of his comments were the sort of things that could only be shouted behind closed doors with the servants sent to the other side of the house. She had behaved like a spoiled child this morning, and one day apart had only made her more vindictive.

Two could play at that game. She had wanted to see him dirty and sweaty and out of sorts. Very well. Here he was, just as she wished. Perhaps he would get drunk as well. Then he would take the carriage and leave her stranded here, begging her friends for a ride home. Perhaps he would even tell Banks to lock the door and go to bed, leaving her sitting on the doorstep until the footman came out to sweep in the morning.

Before he could carry out any part of his plan, he had to find her. It took a few minutes to convince the footman at the door that, despite his appearance, he had been invited to this gathering and was simply arriving late. He also had to face his hostess with sufficient charm to keep her from regretting that she had ever issued him with an invitation.

Only then could he look for Portia. Instead, her mother, or rather, Mrs Braddock found him. She stepped in front of him, blocking his way into the room and said, 'Septon!' as if she had been longing for ages to see him again. She wore the same frigid smile she'd had on his wedding day.

'Madam,' he replied with a nod. He made to go around her.

'My daughter was most kind to share her invitation with me,' she said. 'Since you could not be bothered to bring her here.'

'She did not express such a desire to me,' he said, looking over her head and into the crowd. 'But as you can see, nothing prohibits her from going where she wishes.' The woman was looking at him as if he was keeping her daughter chained in a tower, and he was tired of being polite.

'I suspect, by now, you are tiring of the novelty of marriage,' she said, with a disapproving sniff. 'That is why she had to come here alone tonight.'

'If I was, I certainly would not speak of it with you,' he said, equally cold.

'Portia has no such reservations,' she replied, giving him a smug nod.

'She what?' he snapped.

'She speaks to me often,' she said, laying a hand on the necklace she wore.

Rubies.

So, this was what had happened to the necklace his wife had bought. Apparently she was closer to her poisonous mother than he had known.

Mrs Braddock spoke slowly to make sure he did not miss a word. 'She has had quite enough of your attentions and is longing for the day when she can be sure she is increasing and can get away from you for her confinement.'

It could not be true. She enjoyed his company. She welcomed him enthusiastically to her bed and would follow him to the gates of hell itself if she thought doing so would bring him home.

But how did that explain the damn necklace?

Her mother continued. 'You never wanted this marriage. It was forced upon you. Say the word and my daughter and I will go and leave you to your diversions.'

'Where do you mean to go?' he said, wondering how far their plans had progressed.

'I am sure we can find somewhere that will suit. You have the money to set her up in a house of her own.' She smiled. 'Unless you want to leave the townhouse to her and take an apartment somewhere. I hear the Albany is very fashionable.'

They had barely been together a month, and Portia already wanted to maintain separate households? When she'd first come to him, he had suspected it would happen eventually, after their family was well-established and their interests had diverged.

But that was before he had come to know her. He enjoyed her company and did not want to lose it so soon. Even worse, the thought she could part from him so easily left him too stricken to speak. How had he allowed himself to become bewitched by a woman who wanted nothing to do with him?

He looked past her mother into the ballroom and saw her a few yards away, smiling and waving her fan as if to agree with what her mother was saying. Then she deliberately turned and walked away.

Portia walked across the ballroom, keeping her eyes focused on the man who she might have married, had Julian refused her. She'd seen no difference between the two of them when she'd had the idea to wed. But that was before she'd come to know Julian.

She could not imagine making a life with the stranger that stood in front of her now. He was attractive enough, she supposed, tall and fair and just as elegant as her husband. But when she looked at him, she felt nothing. In return, he was staring at her with a cool curiosity that would have frightened her away, had they been alone in the room.

With the crowd around her and Julian just a few feet away, she was perfectly safe. To prove that she was not bothered, she stared back at him, just as dispassionately, refusing to look away.

When she arrived at his side, he showed no interest in conversation and turned, as if to walk away.

She stepped into his path. 'Going so soon, Your Grace? Has marriage rendered me unworthy of the flatteries that you paid me before the duel?'

'Do I need to gild the lily?' he said, surprised. 'You must know that you are lovely. Or does your husband not tell you so?'

'Let us not speak of Julian,' she said, slipping her hand into the crook of his arm and wondering how long it would take for her husband to come and retrieve her.

'Very well,' he said with a bored sigh. 'What do you wish to speak of instead?'

'Tell me why you fought a duel over me,' she said.

'For the life of me, I have no idea,' he said, staring back. 'The sensible thing to do would have been to retract the things I said about you, since it was obvious they bothered Septon. But he was being such an ass about it that I refused to back down. The next thing

I knew?' He shifted his bad arm and winced. 'I was bleeding on the ground.'

'Surely there is more to it than that,' she said.

'What do you want from me?' he asked, his smile growing by a fraction as his curiosity grew. 'An apology of some sort, I suppose. You must know that I was willing to die rather than give one to your husband.'

'How fortunate for you to be so untroubled,' she said, surprised to feel a faint admiration at his lack of repentance. 'Your actions ruined my reputation, but you are utterly unbothered.'

'My actions?' he said, then shook his head. 'I merely said that you were a fine example of womanhood and I wished it would be possible to know you better.' He smiled. 'I am paraphrasing, of course.'

'Of course,' she agreed.

'Perhaps it was my tone,' he said, then looked her up and down, considering. 'I would still not mind knowing you better.'

The way he said that made the hair stand up on the back of her neck. She should leave immediately, lest people think…

She gave her head a little shake and told herself that scandal no longer mattered. She was married to one of the most scandalous men in London. If that had not already pushed her beyond the pale, nothing would. For the moment, all that mattered was to get

Julian away from her mother before something unforgivable was said.

All the same, she must be careful. She did not know if Westbridge was serious, but she suspected he would take advantage if she let him, just to gain revenge for his wounded arm.

'You know me as well as you are ever going to,' she said, smiling back at him with the same knowing look he was giving her.

He laughed and flexed his weak arm, grimacing in pain. 'It is probably for the best. Casual interest in you has caused no end of trouble thus far. God knows what might happen to me should you take an active interest in our friendship.'

'If you are speaking of my husband?' She shrugged. 'I doubt you have anything to fear. He has no interest in what I do or who I befriend.'

'You wish to be friends with me?' Westbridge said, laughing again. 'Well, now. That is a different matter entirely.'

'Acquaintances,' she allowed, with a smile.

'Even better,' he said, then added, 'Do you know your husband is watching us?' He muttered under his breath, 'Of course you do. That is the point of this conversation, isn't it?'

She shrugged again, then added, 'You owed me something, for causing the duel that ruined my chances.'

'I admit I did mention you to raise his dander. The fellow was annoying me that evening and deserved a little punishment.'

'You thought that a mention of me would hurt him,' she said, with a confused laugh. 'Why?'

He lifted his arm again. 'He was mooning over you at a ball we'd attended, but lacked the nerve to talk to you.'

'Lacked the nerve?' she echoed. 'You are mistaken, Your Grace. My husband would not be put off conversing with a lady, had he a desire to do so. His interest in me was something else entirely.'

'Then you do not know him as well as you think you do,' said Westbridge. 'The fellow was utterly besotted with you, well before the time you married him. It was quite ridiculous.'

'And I say you are mistaken,' she said, still smiling.

'I believe I have already proved my point. Or rather, he did,' he said, shifting his arm again. He glanced past her. 'And here he comes now.'

Without warning, someone took her arm, and she felt an unexpected tingle of excitement, as she did whenever Julian was near. She struggled for a moment to get a hold of her feelings, turning to him with a glittering smile. 'Darling!'

'Hello, my dear,' he responded with a tone that was equally false, the anger under it barely contained.

'I was just speaking with our mutual friend,' she said, daring him to contradict her.

'Westbridge,' he said in an acknowledgement that was full of warning.

'Septon,' the other duke responded with a goading grin. 'I have just been speaking with your charming wife.'

The hand on her arm tightened. 'You have nothing to say to her.'

'On the contrary,' she said, turning to smile at him again. 'We were discussing the duel. As I have been trying to explain to both of you, that is very much my business.'

'That argument has been settled,' her husband reminded her. 'If you wish it to remain so, you had best not stir the pot.'

'Or you could simply learn to control your temper,' she suggested.

'Yes, Julian,' Westbridge said with an overly sweet smile. 'Mind your manners.'

Her husband responded with something that sounded rather like a growl.

She sighed and tugged on his arm. 'The orchestra is tuning up for the waltz and I have no partner.'

'Duty calls,' Westbridge said, and made a shooing gesture at them with his good hand.

With a final venomous look at the man, her husband turned away and led her to the dance floor. As he took her in his arms, she felt the usual rush of desire, which was just as quickly extinguished by the cold look in his eyes.

'What was the meaning of that?' he said, his voice so low that no one but her could hear.

'There was no meaning,' she lied. 'I am acquainted with the Duke. It was only normal that I greet him and wish him well.'

Her husband made a scoffing noise. 'You are lying to me. The one thing I believed, when I agreed to marry you, was that our union would be based on honesty. Tonight has disabused me of that notion.'

She forced a laugh, then sobered, realising such a reaction only proved his point. 'All right. I wished to make you jealous. Did I succeed?'

'That was childish of you,' he replied. 'And most out of character. We agreed when this began that there would be no nonsense about mutual fidelity.'

'That was no answer at all,' she said, thinking of what Westbridge had claimed. If Julian had felt something for her from the start, why would he refuse to show it?

'It is all you are going to receive,' he gritted out.

'Since we agreed that our marriage was never about love, I did not think it would hurt you if I spoke to Westbridge,' she said. 'He is just another man, after all. You have promised that there will be many of those in my future.'

'Perhaps I did not expect the future to begin so soon,' he admitted.

'You mean you thought you would be the one to lose interest in me first,' she said. 'And I see signs of that already.'

'Do you?' His answering smile seemed as dangerous as anything she had seen. Suddenly he spun her so fast she was left giddy and stopped her just as suddenly, reaching out with a hand to stroke her cheek.

Without meaning to, she leaned into the touch, turning just a bit so that the corner of her mouth could reach his fingers as they passed.

His hand was gone just as quickly, and he grabbed her by the upper arms on the bare patches of skin between sleeves and gloves. Then he pulled her close in an open-mouthed kiss, as passionate as anything they'd shared in the bedroom.

In the distance, she heard the music stop, a final violin breaking the silence with a confused squeak that trailed away to nothing. But it did not really matter. Nothing mattered but him.

When he released her, his eyes were blazing, but his expression was just as cold as ever. Without a word, he turned and walked away, leaving her alone in the shocked crowd.

* * *

As he left the house, he passed his own coachman, lounging with his fellows on the corner. The servant jumped to attention, but Julian waved him off and kept walking. The last thing he wanted was another walk. But neither did he wish to leave Portia in a position where she might ask Westbridge for a ride home.

He needed to dispel the rage that was bubbling inside him, and find something that would spend the heat and clear his head. Something outrageous. Something shocking.

The feeling was not unusual. He'd had it many times in the course of his life: this urge to be the mote in his father's eye, the cinder in his shoe. The fact that his father had been dead some five years did nothing to mitigate the desire.

Action helped. So did drinking. He needed to find a pub. Somewhere dark and disreputable that a sane man would avoid. The sort of place where he could get so drunk that he forgot the past and gave no thought to the future. Gin would not solve his problems, but at least he wouldn't feel them for a while.

When she arrived at home later, Portia called Rose to help ready her for bed. When the time came to choose a nightgown, she waved away the more seductive choices in favour of one that was old, worn and familiar. She wanted comfort, and it was not likely she'd get it in the arms of her husband.

She tried not to be nervous. It was doubtful that he was coming home at all, for it was nearly dawn and there had been no sign of him. But to walk back from the edge of the city would take him almost this long, and she could not help hoping that he would arrive, footsore and irritable, right about now.

What if he did? Was she to pretend that nothing had happened? After he had left her, alone on the dance floor, the hush in the room had lasted for what seemed like for ever but was probably only a few seconds. Then people had looked away from her, as embarrassed as she felt by their public display.

This sudden disinterest was almost as bad as overt curiosity. She walked through the crowd of people on the dance floor, the current of conversation swirling around her without quite ever reaching her, until she got to her mother. She gave Portia a triumphant smile, probably convinced that Julian's actions had confirmed her opinion on him. 'Men can be such a burden, my dear. I swear, they call us the weaker sex only to hide their own fractious natures.'

'What did you say to him?' she whispered, dragging her mother to a corner where they could not be overheard.

'Nothing of importance,' her mother replied.

'Did he say anything about your necklace?' she asked.

'Not a word.'

This was good news, she hoped.

'But then, we did not talk for long,' her mother added.

'Did you talk to him about money?' Portia said, squeezing her hands.

'About the future,' her mother corrected. 'And what was to happen once you had his child and could both give up this farce of a marriage.'

'Did he call it that?' she said urgently. 'Was it his plan, or yours?'

'You could not hold him for long,' her mother said, dodging the question. 'You always knew that. But it does not matter. You will still have his name.'

'And his money,' Portia finished for her.

'And that is the most important thing,' her mother finished with a smile. 'Now, enough of this. Let us enjoy the party.'

They stayed for some time after, longer than she'd expected to stay at all, just to prove that her husband's slight had not bothered her. Then she summoned the coach and took her mother home, trying to ignore her endless plans for a future without Julian.

Now she was home herself, alone, her bedroom door open to catch the sound of the opening and closing of the front door. When it came, she went to the head of the stairs and looked down to see her husband in a sorry state, trying with difficulty to make his way past Banks. 'I am just fine,' Julian insisted, patting the butler on the shoulder.

'Of course, Your Grace,' he said with a sigh and pushed Julian towards the stairs and placed his master's hand firmly on the banister.

'I must be very quiet, so I do not wake the household,' Julian said in a stage whisper, then tripped on the first step. He lurched up two more steps, stumbled again and cursed before taking the rest of the flight in an ungainly run.

As he made his way towards her, Portia had time to assess the damage to his person, which was considerable. His boots were muddy from walking, his white breeches stained at the knees from what she assumed was a fall. Or perhaps it had happened during a fight. One of his eyes was black, the bruise extending halfway down his cheek. His coat was ripped at the shoulder and probably quite beyond repair.

She reached for him as he made it to the landing, taking his arm and leading him the last steps to his room.

He waved his hands ineffectually, trying to shake her off. 'I do not need your help.'

'Of course not,' she said, tugging him further into

his bedroom and removing his cravat, which was already untied and flapping against his chest.

'Summon Mason,' he said, then looked past her and bellowed, 'Mason!'

The valet was standing in the doorway of the bedroom, ready to help.

Portia waved him away and eased her husband's coat off his shoulders as he groaned. 'What have you done to yourself?' she murmured, starting on the buttons of his waistcoat.

'I did nothing,' he insisted. 'It was the other fellow.' He touched his eye and winced. 'And you,' he added.

'Me?' she said.

He nodded solemnly. 'You could drive a saint to perdition. What chance did I have?'

'You are talking nonsense,' she said, and turned to Mason. 'Bring ice, and the thistle balm that is in the still room.'

The valet nodded and disappeared.

'Go back to your room, you perfidious wench,' he said, raising an imperious finger and pointing at the connecting door. 'I am fine, I tell you. Just fine.'

'I can see that,' she said dryly.

'And this is all your fault,' he repeated, thrashing out of his waistcoat.

'My fault?' she said, surprised.

'You were talking to that philandering bastard in full sight of everyone.'

'It is far better that I speak to him in public than to seek him out in private,' she said.

'At least you could have waited until you were sure,' he said. 'It has only been a month. How can you be sure?'

She stared at him, waiting for more words that would clarify what he had said, but none came. 'Did my talking with Westbridge really bother you so much?' Perhaps what he had said about Julian being enamoured of her was true.

'You were ready to marry him when you came to me. And now that you are tired of me, you think it is possible to turn back and try again.'

'I only talked to him for a moment and did not mean anything by it,' she said.

'Before you, I had peace,' he said. 'I could do what I wanted.'

'You can do what you want now,' she reminded him. 'I am not stopping you.'

'Because you do not care,' he said.

'I…' Of course she cared. She ached each time he left her. But she had promised that she would not try to change him. 'I do not care,' she repeated, and felt a piece of her heart die.

'And then, you leave me,' he said with a dramatic wave of his hand. 'Going to Westbridge, of all people.'

'I merely talked to him,' she said.

'A first step,' he said ominously.

'If it bothers you so...' Then perhaps she would do it again. She had not expected that tonight's brief conversation would cause such an extreme reaction. She pushed him to sit on the bed and stooped to pull the boots from his feet. 'I will not have a liaison with him,' she promised, since that was an easy enough promise not to break.

'How gracious of you,' he said, fumbling with his breeches buttons as she pulled off his hose. He looked down at her and leered. 'And do not fear that I mean to force my attentions on you. In this condition, I could not do you justice, even if I wanted to.'

'Does that matter so much?' she said, looking up at him.

'I have my reputation as a great lover to consider,' he grumbled, closing his eyes. 'I am the biggest rake in London.'

'Of course you are,' she said, and could not help smiling. 'How could I have forgotten?'

'That is what makes this all so galling,' he said, without explaining what 'this' might be. 'I never suspected, because it has never happened to me before.'

'Then it was probably due,' she said, humouring

him. 'But you needn't worry about it any more tonight.'

'The matter is decided,' he agreed, as Mason appeared to tend to his wounds. 'Go to your room. You have my word that I will not put you out of it. This is your home.'

She laughed and shook her head. 'Go to sleep, Julian. We will talk about it in the morning.'

But when she woke, he was gone.

Chapter Eighteen

The next morning, Julian awoke feeling every minute of the previous day from brain to bone. His feet were blistered from walking, his left cheek throbbed and the eye above it was swollen shut. The crowning glory was the blue-devilled headache behind it. What had made him think that knocking back an inordinate amount of gin in a pub called The Slaughtered Lamb would make anything better?

Probably the same demon that had motivated him to question the parentage of the barkeep when the man had suggested he stop drinking and go home. That had resulted in a black eye and his forcible ejection from the establishment.

It had not been his finest hour.

But it was not every night that a man was informed his wife could not abide his touch and was eagerly awaiting the pregnancy that would free her from it. Then, as if she was already writing the full stop at the end of their marriage, she'd made sure he saw her flirting with Westbridge.

And last night, when he'd come home to confront her, she had not denied any of it.

Of course, his recollection of their conversation was somewhat spotty. But when he'd told her he was ceding the house to her, she'd gone happily off to sleep without another word.

He swung his feet out of bed, wincing again, and rang for Mason, allowing him to shave the unbruised portions of his face and wash away the worst of yesterday's grime. Then he requested that fresh linen and clean shirts be thrown into a valise, took it downstairs, and was out the door without further explanation.

Both Mason and Banks tried to question him on his plans, but he refused them both. For one thing, his wife would have the details out of them if Julian let slip a destination. For another, he had no idea where he was going. Perhaps the Albany, as her shrew of a mother had suggested. But one did not simply appear on the doorstep demanding a set of rooms. An estate agent would be needed.

He considered and rejected the idea of appearing on Cassandra's doorstep and begging for a place to stay. He was paying for the house, after all. Knowing her, she would just laugh and send him straight back to his wife.

In the end, he decided on a room at Grenier's Hotel. It was close to his club and once he was settled there, he wanted to go somewhere well-stocked with brandy, devoid of women and with gentlemen who would mind their own business in regards his injuries.

But when he arrived at the club, there was no sign of the peace he'd been hoping for. As he took his usual seat, he felt a tension in the room that had not been there since the day of the duel.

What had he done, he wondered, to stir up his critics? Had he made the scandal sheets again after his behaviour at the ball last night?

He glanced across the room to see Westbridge, sitting in the bow window. His arm was still in the sling that he'd worn at the ball as he'd talked to Portia. He wore the same chilly smile as well when he turned to focus his attention on Julian.

Julian nodded in acknowledgement and sipped his drink, feeling the held breath around them as the others in the room waited to see if another fight would erupt. If it did, it would not come from him. There was a limit to the number of times in a single day that one behaved like a damned fool, and he had already exceeded his quota.

Westbridge drained his glass before rising and walking across the carpet to take the empty seat opposite him. Then he signalled for another drink and stared at him expectantly. 'Septon,' he said in a neutral tone.

'Westbridge,' Julian said. 'How is the shoulder?'

'Healing nicely,' his opponent said.

'That is good to hear,' he said. Then, unable to help himself, he added, 'If you do not stay away from my wife, I will stab you in the other one.'

At this, his former friend let out a weak laugh, which was followed by a rasping cough.

Julian leaned forward in his chair, no more able to control his worried response than he had been his flash of temper. 'You should not be out yet. You are still not strong enough.'

'I could not abide the sick bed a moment longer,' Westbridge said, taking a sip of his fresh brandy. With the liquor, his colour returned and he relaxed again, looking more like his old self. But not quite the same, for Julian noted the hollows in his cheeks and the way his coat hung loose on his shoulders.

'It is unwise to rush your recovery, all the same,' he muttered, annoyed at the extent of his worry.

'Thank you for your belated concern,' Westbridge replied with an ironic expression. 'You needn't fear that I have come to rekindle our quarrel. I know I am in no condition for another duel.' He added, 'I would not want one, in any case. We have fought enough for one lifetime.'

'You apologise for what you said about her?' he said, trying not to sound as hopeful as he felt.

'I should have done so before,' his friend replied. 'But I did not believe you would be so cloth-brained as to go through with a duel.'

'I am even more stubborn than you are,' he admitted, ignoring the insult. 'And I behaved like a complete fool.'

'You were rather obsessed with the woman who was the source of our argument.'

He opened his mouth to deny it and then stopped himself. To do so would be both a lie and a mistake. He did not want to call attention to his sudden marriage or reveal the reason for it. 'I still am,' he said at last.

Westbridge laughed again and it sounded a little stronger this time. 'I thought so. I have never seen you so hot-headed for such a small reason. Because of that, I could not resist needling you.'

'I almost killed you.' Julian took a deep drink of his brandy, eager to hide how much the truth of that still shook him.

'I have been lying in bed for weeks, trying to decide how I should pay you back,' Westbridge said softly.

'And what is your conclusion?' He had lain awake with a similar thought, though he did not want to admit it.

'That there is no point in seeking revenge. For one thing, I am still too weak to carry it out, and for another, I am more sensible than you and do not see what good it would do to leave the fair Portia a widow.'

'You have expressed your interest in her,' Julian said.

'That was before the duel,' Westbridge pointed out. 'As for last night at the ball?' There was a moment of silence, and then Westbridge smiled. 'I was not the one to approach her, you know.'

'I am aware of that,' Julian admitted. 'I do not really blame you for it. There is not much I can do, if she means to take a lover.' He forced himself to smile as if it did not matter. 'I am tired of playing the fool over a woman.'

Westbridge looked at him with surprise. 'What brought about this change?'

'Marriage,' Julian replied with a sigh.

Westbridge laughed. 'It did not take you long to realise your mistake.'

'And it is not a change,' Julian insisted. 'More like an illness that has passed. I am well again. Back to normal. Even better than I was.' He had Portia to thank for it. His life before her had been one of blissful ignorance, living for pleasure and pretending that nothing mattered. It had all been a lie. He had cared too deeply and acted out of spite. Portia had taught him what it was to feel. Love. Happiness. Connection.

Then she had taken it all from him.

She had shown him his true self, then laughed and walked away. He had thought to be the husband she deserved, but he had been bested at his own game.

'So, my friend,' Westbridge said. 'Now that we have settled our differences and you have cleared your head, what trouble shall we get up to tonight?'

Julian smiled and sipped his drink, trying to fill the emptiness within. 'You choose. It truly does not matter to me.'

When Portia awoke the next morning, she went immediately to Julian's room, expecting to find him still in bed. After the night he'd had, even an insomniac should have been able to manage a few hours of rest. To her surprise, the bed was made and the room empty.

She went down to breakfast and helped herself to tea and eggs, finishing half the plate before she noticed Banks standing in the doorway of the room. Though he was motionless and expressionless, the fact that he dared to interrupt her meal was a sign of extreme agitation.

She put down her fork and looked up at him. 'Was there something you wished to say, Banks?'

'Only that His Grace is gone, Your Grace.'

She frowned. 'He usually is, at this hour.'

'He requested that a bag be packed,' Banks said, his eyebrows raising a fraction of an inch.

'How large a bag?' she asked.

'Linen and shirts for a week,' the butler replied.

'And he did not tell you where he was going?'

'No, Your Grace. Nor did he inform Mason.'

It was probably nothing. But if it was nothing, Banks would not have bothered to tell her so much. 'Has he done this before?' she asked.

'Never, Your Grace.'

'And he said nothing about his plans or his destination.'

The servant shook his head.

Had her brief meeting with Westbridge really upset him so much? She ran back through the conversation they'd had when he'd returned home, searching for something that would explain today's sudden departure. His comments had been rather cryptic, but she'd assumed that had been the liquor talking and that he would be making sense again today.

His last words when she'd put him to bed had been the strangest of all. He had said this was her home and promised not to put her out of her room.

When had this ever been her home? He'd been quite clear when they'd talked about her mother, that this was *his* house, and he would be setting the rules in it. Last night, he had said the matter was settled. The place was hers.

Then he'd packed a bag and left.

She stared at Banks, shocked.

He relaxed ever so slightly as if relieved to see that she finally understood the seriousness of the situation.

It still made no sense. Her talk with Westbridge had been less than five minutes long. That might be reason for an argument, but she could not imagine it causing this unconditional surrender.

Only just before that, he had talked to her mother.

'Banks,' she said, rising from the table. 'Summon the carriage. I am going out.' She hurried to her room to change.

Chapter Nineteen

When they arrived at her mother's house, she signalled the driver to wait and rushed to the front door, pounding on it until the housekeeper let her in. Without waiting for an announcement, she went to the sitting room to find her mother poring over a copy of *Ackermann's Repository*.

'What did you say to him?' she demanded.

'Portia,' her mother said, setting the magazine aside. 'Come, sit down. I will call for tea.'

'What did you say to my husband?' she repeated, her voice shaking with anger.

'Nothing that need concern you,' she said, still smiling. 'I only made an effort to settle our differences.'

'Do not lie to me,' Portia warned.

'It is not a lie,' she insisted. 'We talked about the future.'

'Whose future?' she demanded. 'Yours or mine?'

'All our futures,' she said. 'Once you are with child,

I suggested that he take an apartment, so he might pursue his interests and you yours.'

'I gave you no permission to say such a thing,' she exclaimed, horrified.

'I do not need your permission to say or do what is best for you,' her mother insisted. 'You do not really want to live with him. You only married him so that we might have a secure future. You planned to be free of him once you gave him a son.'

'You told him I no longer wanted him?'

'I told him you never wanted him,' her mother said with a satisfied smile.

'That is not true,' she said in a desperate whisper. 'I love him.'

Her mother shook her head. 'I refuse to believe it. You promised me that you would guard your heart.'

'I love him,' she replied in firm voice, relieved to admit the truth at last.

'The feeling will pass,' her mother said, reaching for the magazine again. 'Now come and look at the latest illustrations in *Ackermann's*. I have some ideas on how we will redo the townhouse, now that we have it to ourselves.'

'No.' Portia took a step back. 'You will not be staying in the townhouse. Julian does not want you there.'

Her mother gave her a disappointed look. 'But, my dear, Julian is not there any more, is he?'

Portia continued to back towards the door. 'He will return.' He had to. She would not lose him this way. 'Even if he does not, I will not have you in my house.'

'Portia!' Her mother gasped. 'Do not speak so.'

'I will speak as I like,' she said. 'And if you come to our townhouse, I will tell the servants to turn you away at the door.' Then she turned and ran for the carriage.

When she got there, she sat for a moment, unsure of what to do next. She needed to find Julian and tell him that it was all a lie. But no one knew where he had gone.

That was not exactly true. He had not told anyone where he was going. But there were places he went regularly, on Wednesdays for example. Why would he need to let an apartment when he had a perfectly good house with a woman who would welcome him any time he arrived?

She knocked on the front wall of the carriage to signal the driver. 'Take me to St John's Wood,' she said. Then she leaned back in her seat, gathering strength for the confrontation that was soon to come.

When they arrived at the house, she did not wait in her seat like the coward she had been, last time. She requested that the step be let down and allowed the coachman to help her to the ground. She walked up to the front door, hesitating only a moment before lifting the knocker and letting it fall.

A moment later, a maid came to enquire after her business.

'I would like to see the lady of the house,' she said, offering her calling card.

'I will see if she is in,' the servant said, smiling as if there was nothing unusual about her presence. She returned quickly and led Portia to a salon. A moment later, the woman she had seen on her last visit appeared in the room. 'Your Grace?' she said with a quizzical smile. 'To what do I owe the pleasure of this visit?'

'I have come to see my husband,' she said, giving the other an unyielding smile.

The woman smiled back, still puzzled. 'You think he is here?'

'Is he not?'

'No,' she replied. 'Nor am I expecting him. Not until Wednesday, at least.'

'Wednesday,' Portia repeated. Portia stood there in silence for a moment, as the dozens of questions about those lost days crowded her mind. Before she could speak, they evaporated like so much smoke. What was she doing here? Her knees went weak. She backed into the nearest sofa and sat down, unable to hold herself up a moment longer. 'It is probably time that we should meet,' she said at last.

'That is very kind of you,' the woman said. 'But I am surprised that, if you wished to meet me, you did not come here with Julian.'

Portia said in a whisper, 'I think…perhaps he would be angry if he knew I was here.'

At this, the woman looked even more puzzled and took a seat opposite her, just as unsure as she was. After a moment's silence, she muttered, 'There should be tea. Would you like tea? Perhaps, it would be easier…'

'Perhaps,' Portia agreed, and for a few minutes her hostess occupied herself with ringing for the maid and ordering refreshments. They sat in awkward silence until the cart appeared and the lady poured for them and offered her cake.

When Portia accepted and agreed that everything was delicious, they realised that they had run out of niceties and were left with silence again. At last, Portia looked to her and said, 'I have one question.'

'Anything,' the woman said, eagerly.

'What is your name?' she whispered.

The woman let out a nervous laugh. 'He has not even told you my name?'

'He has told me nothing, I swear,' Portia said.

'I am Cassandra,' she said. 'Miss Cassandra Fisk.'

'Miss Fisk, I only found you by quizzing the servants about his whereabouts. He has said nothing to me about where he goes.'

'Why would he not tell you?' her hostess said, brows furrowing. 'Do not tell me you are one of those who would look down on me for something that I had no control over at all.'

Perhaps that was true. Not every woman fell from grace because of their own wickedness. She should look to her own brush with infamy and learn something. 'I do not mean to,' Portia said, biting her lip. 'But you see, it was never my intention, but I have fallen in love with him. And the thought that he would spend his afternoons with a mistress and then come home to me as if nothing had happened? I fear it shall break my heart.'

'A mistress?' The other woman's eyes grew wide, and she laughed again, the same incredulous sound she had made before. 'This is all Julian's fault for keeping secrets, and I swear I shall box his ears when next I see him. I am not his mistress.' She shuddered. 'Certainly not.'

'Then who are you?' Portia said, confused.

'His sister. His half-sister, really. Born on the wrong side of the blanket and unacknowledged by our father, but his blood all the same,' she said.

'And Julian visits you every Wednesday,' Portia said numbly.

'Because he is a kind man. He would see me more often, but he fears that his reputation would taint mine,' she said. 'He wants to bring me out in society and to see to it that I meet the right people and have a good future. But he cannot decide how best to go about it. He fears that if I make a sudden appearance on his arm, society might think as you did, that I am merely a mistress passed off as family.'

'That is a problem,' Portia agreed. 'It will take some delicate handling to find a match for you. But with time it can be done.'

'He has been keeping me here in secret until he has formed a plan. He comes here and we talk and play cards and share a meal. It is nothing shocking, really. I do not know why he did not explain to you.'

'Perhaps he does not trust me with the details of his life,' she said, thinking of how few of those he'd shared willingly.

'He is a very private person, even with me,' Cassandra said. 'He does not want others to know what a good man he is.'

'He has the most horrible reputation,' Portia whispered.

'He does not deserve it. He really has been the kindest of brothers,' Cassandra said, smiling fondly. 'He knew our father had a natural child, but did not know what had become of me. When he came into the title, he found the truth of my location written in the old duke's journals.'

'And had you been waiting for him to come for you?' Portia asked.

Cassandra shook her head. 'I was raised in the country and did not know the truth of my parentage until Julian arrived to take me to London.'

'How difficult for you,' Portia replied.

'It was not so bad, really,' the other girl said with a wistful smile. 'I was raised by a vicar and his wife who loved me as their own child and sent me to a good school. I never hoped for anything more than to be a governess. Then Julian came, wanting to make up for our father's neglect.' She sighed. 'He has been very angry with his parents for a very long time. It seems that our father was seen by the *ton* as a paragon of rectitude. But in reality, he was nothing of the sort. When his mother encouraged him to live up to his father's reputation, Julian chose to emulate the darker side of his character to spite them all.'

'That sounds very like him,' Portia admitted. 'He cannot abide hypocrisy. But he is only hurting himself with his behaviour, and I do not think he is particularly happy.'

'He has been much better, since he got married,'

Cassandra said with a smile. 'He speaks of you often and has been quite distracted on our recent visits. I think he would rather be at home with you.'

'Until yesterday, perhaps,' Portia said. 'There has been a misunderstanding between us. And now he is gone and I have no idea where.'

'Not far, I am sure,' Cassandra said. 'He would not leave London without telling me. I suggest you send a servant around to the best hotels. You will likely find him sulking in one of them.'

'Thank you,' Portia said, reaching out to take her hand before rising to leave. 'When I have found him and settled things, we will have a talk about how best to handle your future.'

'That would be most helpful,' Cassandra said, escorting her to the door. 'Now go and find your husband. I am sure the trouble between you will be easily settled.'

'I pray you are right,' she said, and hurried back to the carriage.

Chapter Twenty

It was barely midnight when Julian returned to his hotel room, the earliest he'd gone to bed in ages.

The earliest he'd gone to bed alone, at least. There had been many even earlier nights since he'd married Portia. But he had promised himself that he would not be thinking of them, or of her. The knowledge that she'd been biding her time until he would leave her alone tainted all the pleasant memories and left him wishing that the whole of the last month could be excised from his memory.

He could not even find pleasure in his usual haunts, for she'd spoiled those as well. Westbridge had suggested gambling, and he'd thought of her at The Inferno, fleecing strangers at piquet. When he'd refused, Westbridge had claimed a girl would take his mind off his troubles, and that had reminded him of the erotic interlude in the carriage.

How had she managed to leave her mark on each

corner of his life, rendering inferior things that had once been pleasurable? After last night, he did not even want to get drunk. The swelling over his eye had gone down somewhat, but he still felt like a stewed owl. There was nothing for it but an early night in a strange bed, where he would probably lie awake thinking of a woman who, according to her mother, wanted nothing to do with him.

He trudged up the stairs to the room he'd let, which was on the third floor and opened the door to find a footman in Septon livery lounging in a chair by the bed. To his annoyance, the boy did not leap to his feet when discovered. Instead, he tipped his tricorn forward and grinned.

'Here, you,' Julian barked. 'What is the meaning of this? Did my wife send you? Because we have nothing more to say to each other.'

'Is that so, Your Grace?' the knave replied in a voice that took his breath away.

He stared for a moment before snatching the hat away and knocking the powdered wig askew. 'Portia?'

She plucked the wig off and dropped it on a nearby table, smiling up at him. 'Close your mouth before you catch a fly, Julian. And close the door as well.'

He eased it shut behind him, leaning against it and continuing to stare. 'What is the meaning of this costume?'

'This is a decent hotel that will not let a female into the room of a male guest, even if she claims to be his wife,' she said. 'But a servant in the man's own livery can pass unnoticed.'

Unnoticed was probably an exaggeration. When she stood up to show him the effectiveness of her disguise, he could barely pull his eyes away from her shapely calves covered in nothing but cotton hose and the way the leather knee breeches clung to her thighs and bottom. 'That is indecent,' he said.

'Is it?' she said, sitting down in a way that was both unladylike and ungentlemanly. 'I find it all very liberating.'

'Never mind,' he said, covering his eyes. 'Just tell me why you are here.'

'I came to inform you that my mother is a terrible liar, and that you should pay her no mind,' she said, still smiling.

'Your mother...' He stopped, for though he'd vowed to forget what she had said to him, every word of the conversation was clear in his head. 'She was wearing your rubies,' he said.

'Her rubies,' Portia replied. 'She went shopping for herself and sent the bills to you.'

'At your instruction?' he asked.

'I paid her creditors with the money from your

study,' she admitted. 'But the later purchases were her own idea.'

'You want me to support her,' he argued.

'I do,' she said. 'But that does not mean I wish her to live in your house or run up expenses in your name.' Now she looked at him with what seemed to be remorse. 'She is my mother, and I love her despite everything. But I had no idea she would come to you, telling such awful lies and trying to ruin things between us. Really, this has very little to do with you at all. She is still angry at Father.'

'He has been gone for well over a year,' Julian said.

'But you are still alive to bear his punishment. I am sorry. Truly I am.' She laid a hand across her waistcoated breasts and let out a sigh of relief. 'I feel so much better, now that I have told you. You have no idea.'

'And what lies has she told me?' he said, glancing down at her legs again, then steeling his resolve. 'You married me for my title and my money. You swore you did not care about me.'

'That was true at first,' she agreed. 'But things changed quite quickly. And when I thought you were visiting a mistress…'

'I have no mistress,' he said.

'Cassandra,' she said, waving her hand. 'You really should have told me about her. But you never told me anything. And you kept leaving on Wednesdays with wine and a hamper. What was I to think?'

'You know about Cassandra?' he said, trying to keep up with the torrent of information that was pouring from her.

'I bullied the coachman into telling me your Wednesday destination. And yesterday, I was so angry with you that I decided to look for you there. And I only talked to Westbridge to stop you from talking to Mother.' She took a breath. 'But it was too late.'

He was silent for a moment, picking and choosing from the statements, trying to decide which of them mattered. Then he chose his favourite. 'You were upset when you thought I had a mistress.'

'Livid,' she replied.

'Jealous?'

'Madly so,' she agreed.

'You promised you would not care where I went or what I did,' he reminded her.

'And I have failed, miserably,' she said with a shrug. Beneath the wool uniform, her breasts shifted in a way that made him suspect she had not bothered with stays.

'Tell me more,' he said, removing his hat and gloves.

'You should have told me about your sister,' she said, giving him a stern look.

He should have. But he had not been able to imagine wanting to share his life so completely with another human being. A lot had changed in a month. 'I am sorry,' he said, surprising himself with the words and even more with the fact that he meant them.

'I forgive you,' she said.

The feeling of relief that followed her words was yet another surprise.

'I have been giving the matter much thought while waiting for you to come back here,' she said. 'I think I could help you with introducing her into society.'

'You have barely made your own mark there,' he said.

'Because I have not tried very hard,' she reminded him. 'I am not mad for parties and balls, as some women are.'

'You are not?' he said, surprised yet again.

'Not really. But if we were to go out more often, and you were to curtail your usual evening entertainments in favour of more staid pursuits, it would do much to improve your reputation. Perhaps we should sponsor a charity together.'

'A school for wayward girls?' he suggested.

She snorted. 'I think not. A hospital or an orphanage. Something that would put your money to good use and cement you as an altruist in the public eye.'

'And the purpose of that would be?'

'To keep you so busy that you have no time to get

into trouble,' she said, beaming at him. 'And to make it so that no one questions you when we introduce your sister Cassandra onto the marriage mart.'

'You are planning each detail of the rest of my life,' he said, surprised once again that the prospect did not bother him one bit.

'For the sake of your sister,' she said, looking so innocent that he could almost believe her.

'No,' he said, and watched her face fall. Then he added, 'If you had another reason for wanting such changes? If you loved me, perhaps…'

'Maybe I could not stand the thought of you, out every night and not in my bed?' she suggested.

He grabbed her by the hand and pulled her up out of the chair and against his body. 'Say the words,' he whispered. 'The ones you know I want to hear.'

'I love you,' she said sincerely. 'I never meant to. But I do.' She slipped her arms beneath his coat and hugged him about the waist. 'And do you have anything to say to me?' she coaxed.

'I do,' he said. 'You are wearing far too much clothing. I can hardly feel you through the coat. And the breeches…' The breeches were a different matter entirely. He let his hands stray, investigating them.

She made a pouting noise but did not resist.

'Ah, yes,' he said, gathering his thoughts. 'You want to know how I feel.'

'Do not torture me,' she said, wriggling against him.

'I love you, as well,' he said, kissing the centre of her lower lip to chase away her frown. 'Have loved you from the first moment I saw you.' He ran his hands over her hips, down her leather-clad legs. The sensation was unfamiliar and very arousing. 'Why couldn't it have been lust?' he muttered, cupping her bottom. 'I understand lust.'

'You do,' she agreed, reaching between them to undo some buttons.

'But I know nothing about being a loving husband,' he said.

'You will learn,' she said.

'I will,' he agreed, pulling her hips into his. 'But not before I do something very wicked to you.'

'I was hoping you would,' she murmured.

And then, neither of them said anything at all.

Epilogue

'Do you think there are enough flowers?' Portia stared at the walls of the hired assembly room and the garlands of greenery and deep purple hellebores that swagged between the windows.

'There can never be too many,' her mother said, casting a critical eye on the decorations. 'But what you have done is very nice. I have never seen anything quite like it.'

'If I am having the first ball of the Season, I want it to be memorable,' Portia replied with a smile.

'It is a shame that Septon's townhouse does not have a ballroom of its own,' her mother said, her lips pursing slightly.

'But there is nothing we can do about that,' Portia said firmly, and watched as her mother nodded in agreement. She still had a tendency to be critical where Julian was concerned, but it was nowhere near as bad as it had been eight months ago, when they had first married.

After the incident at the Hackville ball, Portia had refused to speak with her until she'd apologised to Julian and promised there would be no more tricks. In turn, he'd agreed to take on her expenses and provided her with an allowance that was so generous her feelings towards him had softened.

Now she seemed more concerned with the lack of a grandchild than her son-in-law's former reputation as one of London's most scandalous gentlemen.

Without thinking, Portia laid a hand on her stomach, letting it drop before her mother remarked on it. It was only a month since she'd missed her courses, but it was quite possible that her mother's final criticism would be settled in around seven months' time.

'Where is Septon?' she asked, glancing towards the door.

'He has gone to get Cassandra and the Fisks. They should all be here directly,' Portia said. 'The ball cannot begin without them, after all.'

'It was very sensible of your husband to include Reverend Fisk in the planning of the school he is sponsoring,' her mother said with surprising forbearance.

'The vicar and his wife did a fine job of raising and educating Cassandra,' Portia replied. 'They deserved a reward of some kind. The position as headmaster at the new Septon school suits him well. And combining the charity ball with Cassandra's first public appearance will make a happy night for all of us.'

As she had expected, the door to the hall opened and Reverend and Mrs Fisk appeared. They looked about them in awe at the decorations and the crystal punch bowls and towers of wine glasses ready for chilled champagne.

Portia greeted them, introducing them to her mother, and turned to welcome her husband, who entered with his sister on his arm. Cassandra was radiant in a white ball gown and wearing the amethyst and diamond necklace that she and Julian had chosen from the lock room at his country home.

Not only was it a perfect match for the flowers that decorated the room, it was a family piece that had belonged to Julian's grandmother. It would be easily recognised as belonging to the Parish entail and would announce to one and all that Cassandra was truly a member of the family.

But, as it usually was, the diamonds Portia was wearing were a recent gift. When Julian had explained his hatred for his mother's jewellery collection, they'd agreed to reset the entailed pieces and sell those that had no significance, using the proceeds to fund the school. If the gossips had anything to say about the new jewellery that Portia always seemed to have, it was that Septon had exceptional taste and was as generous with his wife as his father had been with his mother.

After a turn around the room to see the decorations, Cassandra left her brother and came to take Portia's hand. 'This night is more wonderful than I ever imagined it could be. I do not know how I can ever thank you.'

'There is no need,' Portia replied. 'We are sisters now, are we not?'

'And we want you to find someone who will make you as happy as we are,' Julian said, stepping forward to give Portia a welcome kiss. Then he turned back to Cassandra. 'Why don't you speak to the orchestra leader. If you have favourite pieces of music, we want to be sure he plays them all for you.'

She gave him a dazzled smile and a kiss on the cheek and then ran off to do as he suggested, leaving Portia and Julian alone together.

They smiled at each other in silence for a moment and then Julian stepped behind her, wrapping his arms about her and kissing the side of her neck.

'Gently.' She laughed. 'I cannot be greeting the cream of London society with love bites on my throat.'

'As long as they know who gave them to you, I see no problem.'

'Of course you don't. You are incorrigible.'

'Me?' he said, as his breath tickled her ear. 'Do not say so. If I were irredeemable, I would not be counting the hours until I can go home to bed, with my wife.'

She giggled and pretended to pull away from him. 'If you are marking time, then you will see that it is not yet eight and the festivities will not end until near to dawn.'

'Dawn?' He yawned. 'Woman, you will be the death of me. I have not been up so late in ages.'

'What happened to the man I married?' she said with a mock sigh.

'I hardly recognise him myself,' he admitted and gave her another kiss. 'Sensible. Sober. Sleeping through the night. I am a shadow of my former self.'

'Well, you must pull yourself together for a couple of hours,' she said. 'Tonight, you must charm your friends out of their money in the card room.'

'For the good of uneducated orphans,' he said.

'And dance with me until dawn,' she added. 'If I can survive a late night, in my delicate condition, so can you.'

'Delicate? You're...' He pulled away from her and spun so he could look into her eyes.

She touched a finger to his lips to stop his speech. 'We will discuss it later, at home, when we are alone. But yes, I think so.'

He kissed her gently, but with the skill of a man

who knew her better than she did herself. Then he said, 'Until then, it will be our secret. For now? Let us open the doors and begin the music. Tonight, we will make memories.'

'Tonight and every night,' she said, as they went to greet their guests.

* * * * *

*If you enjoyed this story, be sure to read
Christine Merrill's
previous Historical romances*

A Scandalous Match for the Marquess
A Duke for the Penniless Widow
Awakening His Shy Duchess
How to Survive a Scandal
Lady Rachel's Dangerous Duke

MILLS & BOON®

Coming next month

HIS CINDERELLA DUCHESS
Tina Gabrielle

Brent leaned forward in his chair. 'You do recall the arrangement you proposed? You want a child. I need an heir for the dukedom. For either to happen, we have to share a bed.'

She felt her cheeks burn hot. She was by no means blind to his attractiveness. Still, mention of bedchamber visits made her heart thump hard in her chest. 'I understand but I still want a proper courtship.'

'How long?'

'Three months from the wedding.' She knew this was lengthy but meant it to be a point of negotiation.

He shook his head. 'A week.'

'A month.'

'A week.'

She pushed back her chair and stood. 'You are being inflexible. However, since the banns of marriage must be read aloud in church for three Sundays prior to the wedding, I'll agree to a three week courtship.'

He rose, walked around his desk and stopped before her. She stood her ground and raised her chin, trying to assess his unreadable features. To her surprise, an unwelcome surge of excitement at his nearness made her pulse leap.

He leaned casually against the desk. 'Banns are not required if a special license is obtained.' His voice was level.

She gaped. 'A special license? But…but that requires the Archbishop's consent himself.'

'I know.' An unmistakable hint of arrogance tinged his voice.

Continue reading

HIS CINDERELLA DUCHESS
Tina Gabrielle

Available next month
millsandboon.co.uk

Copyright © 2025 Tina Sickler

COMING SOON!

We really hope you enjoyed reading this book. If you're looking for more romance be sure to head to the shops when new books are available on

Thursday 28th August

To see which titles are coming soon, please visit
millsandboon.co.uk/nextmonth

MILLS & BOON

afterglow BOOKS

Afterglow Books is a trend-led, trope-filled list of books with diverse, authentic and relatable characters, a wide array of voices and representations, plus real world trials and tribulations. Featuring all the tropes you could possibly want (think small-town settings, fake relationships, grumpy vs sunshine, enemies to lovers) and all with a generous dose of spice in every story.

@millsandboonuk
@millsandboonuk
afterglowbooks.co.uk
#AfterglowBooks

For all the latest book news, exclusive content and giveaways scan the QR code below to sign up to the Afterglow newsletter:

SCAN ME

FOUR BRAND NEW BOOKS FROM
MILLS & BOON MODERN

The same great stories you love, a stylish new look!

WED IN A HURRY
KIM LAWRENCE — LORRAINE HALL
2 BOOKS IN ONE

Bound & Crowned
LOUISE FULLER — CLARE CONNELLY
2 BOOKS IN ONE

Love to HATE HIM
JULIA JAMES — MILLIE ADAMS
2 BOOKS IN ONE

RECLAIM ME
CATHY WILLIAMS — DANI COLLINS
2 BOOKS IN ONE

OUT NOW

Eight Modern stories published every month, find them all at:
millsandboon.co.uk

LET'S TALK
Romance

For exclusive extracts, competitions and special offers, find us online:

- **f** MillsandBoon
- **X** @MillsandBoon
- **O** @MillsandBoonUK
- **d** @MillsandBoonUK

Get in touch on 01413 063 232

For all the latest titles coming soon, visit
millsandboon.co.uk/nextmonth